Winner Books are produced by Victor Books and are designed to entertain and instruct young readers in Christian principles. Each book has been approved by specialists in Christian education and children's literature. These books uphold the teachings and principles of the Bible.

Bernard Palmer of Holdrege, Nebraska is well-known as a story teller. He's been writing stories with a Christian message since 1940—books and articles for children, teens, and adults. The Danny Orlis books, done for "Back to the Bible" broadcast, are probably the best known. He has written over 270 books and more than 500 articles and short stories.

Bernie started Kearney Teacher's College in Nebraska with hopes of becoming a lawyer. But after only a year, he had to leave college because of the lack of money. He went to work in his father's tombstone shop in Holdrege and labored there for many years. He and his wife work together, writing. This is his first Winner Book.

Ted and the Secret Club

Bernard Palmer

illustrated by Joe Van Severen

A WINNER BOOK

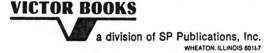

VICTOR BOOKS

a division of SP Publications, Inc.

WHEATON. ILLINOIS 60187

Offices also in Fullerton, California • Whitby, Ontario, Canada • Amersham-on-the-Hill, Bucks, England

Library of Congress Catalog Card Number: 79-67407
ISBN: 0-88207-487-3

VICTOR BOOKS
A division of SP Publications, Inc.
P.O. Box 1825, Wheaton, Illinois 60187

CONTENTS

Ted Performs for the Rangers

TED WILLS HURRIED to his grandmother's house after school and snatched up a grocery sack. In it were two of his most precious magic tricks. The clock on the kitchen wall told him he was already 20 minutes late. Miss Winslow, his sixth-grade teacher, had asked him and another boy to stay and help her move her desk.

The other Rangers would be waiting for him in Bart Harrison's basement. Since Ted was president, they couldn't start without him.

He was about to burst out into the biting November wind again when Grandma Mason's shrill voice stopped him. "Ted!" she called from her rocker near the oil burner in the living room.

"Yes, Grandma," he answered.

"Be sure to button your coat tight. And don't forget, supper is at 6 o'clock."

Ted assured her that he would do as she asked and hurried out. His mind was on the meeting and the sack in his hand. He hadn't said anything to the Rang-

7

ers or anyone else about the magic tricks his Uncle Carl gave him when he and his mother and Anne were out at the ranch last winter. But he had been working with them at home, sharpening his skills. Now he felt the time had come for him to show off his new ability.

He buttoned up his jacket as he ran down the alley behind Grandma's place, then crossed a vacant lot to the Harrison's.

Bart's mother was expecting him. She was a bustling, red-faced woman with a friendly smile. Her kitchen usually smelled of rising bread, cinnamon rolls, doughnuts, cookies, or pies. "The boys are in the basement, Ted," she told him.

He gave her a quick smile and hurried past to the door that led downstairs.

Bart met him at the bottom step, his broad face serious. "Boy, Miss Winslow sure kept you long enough!"

Ted nodded. "Heavy desk," he said breathlessly.

"Come on in and close the door."

Ted sat down on the rug and leaned against the cold wall, facing his friends, and took a deep breath. He decided to start right away since they were late.

"Anybody here followed to our secret meeting place?" he asked. "Bart?" Bart shook his head. "Loren?"

"Nope," Loren replied.

"Dave?" He shook his head too.

For a while they talked about the secret code they were working on. When they had the code perfected, they'd be able to write messages to each other, and nobody else would be able to read them.

Then Bart asked, "Ted, what's going to happen when your mom and Mr. Denholm get back?"

"Yeah, what's going to happen?" Dave put in. "About our club. You'll still be a member, won't you?"

Ted began to get warm. He pushed his sand-colored hair off his face. "I don't see what Mom's marriage has to do with our club. After all, the club was my idea. Sure, Anne and I will be moving to the Denholm farm with Mom, but that shouldn't change our club."

No one said anything for a couple of minutes. Then Dave asked, "What about Cliff?"

"He won't find out any Rangers' secrets from you, will he?" Bart asked.

"Yeah, he'll be your brother," Loren said.

Ted was stunned. It was no secret that he didn't like his new stepbrother, Cliff Denholm. Cliff was a year older but in sixth grade with them. He was pushy and could be mean. For some reason, he wanted to join the Rangers. He'd even offered Dave his jackknife if Dave would get him into their club.

"Look, I was the one who didn't want him in our club. Do you think I'll blab our secrets to him?" Ted answered.

"But what about that sister of his?" Bart wanted to know.

"Anita?" Ted frowned and took his jackknife from his pocket and fingered it.

Anita Denholm was a year younger—in fifth grade. She was a thin, lively tomboy who could climb trees and play baseball better than most guys. She was easily the fastest kid in school and often won games like "Pump Pump, Pull Away" or "King of the Mountain." If there was a kite contest, hers was sure to be a winner.

Although Ted would never admit it to the Rangers —he was proud she was going to be his sister. It was just too bad she was a girl.

"What about her?" Ted asked, defensively.

"You know what the rules say about girls," Bart said. "A guy's not supposed to be around them or carry their books or walk home with them."

"But sisters don't count," Loren countered. He had three sisters of his own.

Ted agreed. He hadn't been around Anita all that much, but he had to put up with Anne; so he was used to girls.

"But she's not his real sister," Bart protested, as though that ought to make a difference.

"She's the same as his real sister," Loren put in. "They'll be living in the same house."

They talked for some time before deciding that it would be all right for their club president to be around Anita, since he couldn't very well avoid her. But they were also concerned about his letting her know any of their secrets. That would ruin everything.

"You don't have to worry," Ted said. "I know how to keep my mouth shut."

They were about to adjourn when Ted remembered his sack. "Just a minute," he said. "I have something to show you. When I was way out in the panhandle of

Nebraska, I got to know a magician. He got his tricks from an old, old man. Then he gave them to me."

The Rangers eyed him doubtfully and Bart said, "Come off it, Ted! Don't try to give us that stuff!"

"Yeah," Dave added. "You're no magician."

"That's what you think," Ted said.

"OK, if you're so smart, show us!" Bart challenged.

That was exactly what he'd been waiting for. "It so happens that I have some of my tricks right here." He opened the bag and got out the magic wand Uncle Carl had given him. "Now watch carefully," he urged them.

They stared at him unbelievingly as he performed. Afterward, Loren said, "How'd you do that?"

He shook his head. "Sorry, I gave my word that I wouldn't tell anyone how to do any of the tricks."

"But we're all Rangers!" Dave protested. "We're not supposed to have secrets from each other."

"I can't tell you guys—or anyone else," Ted answered. "I gave my word before Uncle Carl would tell me any of his secrets."

They were not about to accept that, but Mrs. Harrison knocked on the door just then and announced that it was after 5:30, so the boys hurried upstairs.

The kitchen was warm and cheery with its delicious smells of baked things. She gave them each a fresh cinnamon roll then bundled them out into the darkening night to hurry home.

Ted got back to Grandma's just as she was putting supper on the table. After they finished eating, he and 13-year-old Anne sat in the kitchen with her and listened to "Amos 'n' Andy" and "Lum and Abner," so popular in 1933, on the crackling radio.

Then it was time for dishes. Once they were done, Ted and Anne went into the living room and sat, cross-legged on the floor in front of Grandma's old rocker while she read to them from the Bible.

She read about love from 1 John and talked to them earnestly about pleasing the Lord Jesus. "We should try to get along with people and have love and consideration for them." Her lined face was drawn with emotion as she spoke.

She didn't tell them what she was referring to, but they both knew. By the end of the week they would be moving from their home in Elmville to the Denholm farm, about three miles out. To be sure, they were not moving far. They would still attend the same school and church, but things would be different. They had already become aware of that. Things had been different from the time their mother started seeing Mr. Denholm.

As soon as Grandma finished evening devotions, Anne got to her feet. "Come on, Ted," she said. "Let's go into the kitchen and study."

"Are you sure you feel all right, Anne?" Grandma asked.

"That's what I was wondering," Ted said, laughing. "You've never asked me to study with you before."

"Oh, c'mon, you two," Anne protested.

"You do look sort of tired, Anne," Grandma continued, "and I thought I heard you wheezing while I was reading."

"I might be wheezing a little," Anne admitted, shrugging. "I'll go and get my medicine."

"I think I'd better fix you a bed on the couch in the living room so you'll be close to the heater," Grandma told her. "It's too cold for you to sleep in that bedroom upstairs. I don't want you having a bad attack of asthma while you're here."

Anne protested, but Grandma was not to be persuaded. "You and Ted can go in the kitchen and study. I'll get some sheets and blankets so you can make yourself a bed down here." She got painfully to her feet and hobbled into the bedroom on the main floor.

"Come on," Anne urged her brother. "I want to talk to you."

Still grumbling, he gathered up his books and followed her to the table in the large, friendly kitchen. "I didn't think you wanted me to study with you," Ted said.

She moved closer and lowered her voice. "It's about you and Clifford Denholm—you might as well know. Grandma asked me to talk to you."

Ted rolled his eyes upward and made a helpless gesture.

"Ted, you've got to promise to get along with him —for Mom's sake."

Ted's brown eyes narrowed. "Why don't you talk to Cliff?" he asked irritably. "He's the one who's always pushing little kids around and lying and stuff. Let me clue you. If he and I have any trouble, it'll be his fault, not mine."

"It takes two to fight," Anne reminded him.

Ted drew himself up. "Not if one guy's Cliff Denholm!"

"Grandma says she was talking to Cliff's aunt about him," Anne continued. "He wasn't like he is now, before his mother died. After her death, he started acting loud and mean. She said she feels sorry for him."

"Great! Then let her and Grandma look after him," Ted exploded.

Anne reached out impulsively and grasped his arm. "Please, Ted." Her wheezing suddenly got worse, and she had a fit of coughing that shook her thin body. Ted had seen it happen hundreds of times, it seemed, but it always scared him.

It was a moment or two before she could speak again. "Ted, please. You're supposed to be a born-again Christian."

He frowned angrily. He could think of a lot of things to say, but he was afraid he would only make her asthma worse.

"Promise me you'll be good to him," she persisted.

"Why don't you get him to promise to be good to me?" he countered.

"Ted!" she pleaded.

He knew he had to agree or she'd keep hounding him. "Oh, OK," he said. "I'll do what I can."

She smiled gratefully. "Thanks," she said softly. "I could kiss you!"

"Watch it!" he exclaimed quickly, drawing away. "And you better take that medicine of yours."

He didn't think they had been talking loudly enough for Grandma to hear, but she must have guessed that the conversation was over. She called out loudly for him to go upstairs to bed, reminding him that he had school the next day.

He went up to the cold room, still fuming. He had had his share of trouble too! It hadn't been easy on him, having his dad die when he was only eight. But nobody thought about that. And now he had to pussy-foot around Cliff Denholm because Cliff had lost his mama. "Big baby!" Ted sputtered.

He undressed hurriedly and crawled between the sheet blankets, shivering. Two more nights at Grandma's and they'd be moving out to the Denholm farm.

He stared blankly up at the ceiling. Now that his eyes had grown used to the darkness, he was able to make out the naked light bulb suspended from a short length of insulated wire and the frame of the small picture on the wall above the iron bedstead. Ted couldn't distinguish the likeness in the photograph, but he didn't have to. He had seen it many times. It was a faded photo of Grandma's father. Great Grandfather was a stern individual with whiskers and piercing eyes that looked as though they didn't know what it was like to smile.

Ted had always felt uncomfortable in the room with those eyes watching everything he did. He had, that is, until Grandma told him the story. Her pa, as she called him, had been killed by a buffalo over on the Republican River, south of their homestead.

The huge buffalo had been in with the cattle. Grandpa had gone out to shoot him or drive him away. The old muzzle-loading rifle misfired, and the buffalo charged and gored Grandpa to death. Ted was so proud, he even took the Rangers up to see the picture and had Grandma tell them how Grandpa got killed.

Now he enjoyed sleeping in the old iron bed beneath the picture. He would put himself to sleep, imagining he had been there with Grandpa Parker when he went to chase the buffalo away. Only the way he imagined it, he had a rifle too. When Grandpa's rifle didn't go off, he shot and wounded the bull buffalo. It almost killed him with its horns before it fell dead, but he saved Grandpa Parker's life.

It was different that night, however. He was so troubled, he only thought about Grandma's pa and the buffalo for a couple of minutes. He didn't even get to the part where the rifle misfired. Moving out to the farm and having to live with a creep like Cliff wasn't going to be easy.

He thought about what Anne had said. Maybe Cliff had been different before his mother died, maybe not quite as mean. But his mother had spoiled him. The kids all knew that. And he sure could be nasty now!

Last winter Ted had caught Cliff grabbing money from the 8-year-old Arnold twins. Cliff had always kind of competed with Ted in school. Cliff was older and bigger, but Ted was smarter. But since Ted turned him in for stealing from the twins, he'd really had it in for Ted.

Why, oh why had his mother fallen in love with Wilber Denholm, Cliff's dad—of all people? Of course,

Mr. Denholm was OK. Ted knew he'd enjoy living with the tall, soft-spoken farmer. His features were ruddy and scarred by wind and sun. True, he didn't have much money. But nobody did since the Depression and drought had hit.

Ted rolled over on his side once more and closed his eyes. At least Mom had been a lot happier since she and Mr. Denholm had started seeing each other. That meant a lot!

Before dropping off to sleep, Ted prayed for Grandma and Anne and Mom and Mr. Denholm—and Anita. He prayed for the Rangers too and asked God to help him live the way a Christian should. But he didn't pray for Cliff—not right then. He just couldn't.

Two Families 2 Become One

MR. DENHOLM and Ted's mother came home on November 7, a Friday afternoon, and both families gathered as one around the supper table that evening at Grandma Mason's. After eating, Ted's mom took her two children aside privately and asked them to call Mr. Denholm "Dad." But they didn't know if they could do that. It didn't seem right when they could still remember their own father.

"We could call him 'Uncle Wilber,'" Ted suggested.

"But he's not our uncle!" Anne retorted, scornfully.

"He's not our dad, either," Ted replied.

So, there the matter stood.

Saturday was moving day. Ted and Anne went home from Grandma's shortly after breakfast to find Mr. Denholm already at their house with his truck. Anita and Cliff had come along and were helping take the furniture out of the house and load it.

Cliff scowled as Ted approached. "Where've you been?" he grumbled. "You were supposed to be here, helping. Part of this junk's yours, you know."

Ted was about to make an angry reply, but Anne caught his eye and warned him to be silent with a frown and shake of her head. He turned from his new stepbrother and went into the house where his mother was directing the job of taking apart the beds, removing pictures from the walls, and packing dishes.

He began to carry boxes out to the truck, meeting Cliff in the now empty living room. The other boy glared at him, but said nothing. Ted brushed past, trying to keep his own thinly veiled hostility from showing. He didn't know how such a nice guy as Wilber Denholm could have a kid like Cliff. Ted was beginning to wonder why he had ever promised Anne he'd be nice to Cliff. No matter what Ted did, Cliff would see to it that they weren't friends. That's the way it had been at school, anyway.

Ted could have used some help, carrying out the box of magic tricks his uncle had given him. But he struggled with it alone. Cliff had performed magic in the all-school chautauqua (program) for two years. Ted didn't want Cliff to know he was interested in magic now too. But just as Ted was putting the box on the truck, the bigger boy came up.

"Hey, what've you got there?" Cliff asked, curiously.

Ted could feel his cheeks getting warm. "Some personal stuff," he muttered.

Cliff flipped the padlock and made a face. "It must be something valuable to have it locked up as tight as that."

"It is," Ted answered. The instant he spoke he realized he had made a mistake. To tell Cliff it was valuable might be enough to get him snooping around to find out what was in the box, and he didn't want that. "It is valuable," he repeated, "to me."

"What is it? Love letters?" Cliff teased.

Ted managed a thin laugh.

"You'll have to let us read 'em some time," Cliff added.

They set back to work, and Ted hoped that was the end of Cliff's curiosity about the big box. Still, he planned to keep it in a safe place and be sure it was always locked.

The truck was loaded and about to leave for the farm when Ted finally got up courage to ask Mr. Denholm about taking along his basketball goal. He had earned the money for the goal and his new ball by picking up—he didn't know how many—pop bottles at 2¢ each.

He wanted to take the goal out to the farm almost as much as he wanted his magic tricks. He had thought about it first thing that morning, but he hadn't known whether Mr. Denholm would want to be bothered. Nervously, he mentioned it.

"Sure thing, Ted," his stepfather said, kindly. He went back to the truck and got the ladder he had just put on. "We'll get it down in a jiffy."

Ted smiled his gratitude. That only proved that he had been right about Mr. Denholm all along. "D—do you think there might be a place we can put it up at the farm?" he asked. "Where it wouldn't be in the way?"

"No problem. As soon as we get this stuff unloaded,

we'll look for a place to put up your goal. How about that?" Mr. Denholm said, smiling.

Ted knew, then, if he hadn't known before, that he and his mother's new husband would get along fine.

* * *

He had been out on the Denholm farm two or three times before, but he had never really seen it the way he did that morning. The house was set back from the road a quarter of a mile or so. It was approached by a long lane bordered with cottonwood trees.

The two-story house was as bare and gray as the desolate fields that surrounded it. The siding still carried the faint markings of white paint that years of rain and snow and blowing dust hadn't nibbled away. The gate in the backyard fence leaned on its post like an old man on his cane.

Windows in the kitchen looked out on the large, broad-beamed barn. On one side of the barn stood a machine shop. On the other side were two smaller buildings. Behind them all towered the windmill.

They unloaded the truck and hauled the furniture inside. Ted's mom had only kept a few pieces, but they were enough to crowd both the living and dining rooms. Cliff grouched about it, but only loud enough for Ted to hear. There were no real problems, however, until Mr. Denholm told Ted to take his things up to Cliff's room. Cliff followed Ted upstairs, angrily.

"Which one's your room?" Ted asked, glancing around uneasily as he reached the top of the stairs. He had to *room* with Cliff, no less!

His companion frowned. "Why?"

Ted sighed. "Because your dad said I was supposed to put my stuff there."

For an instant the air between them was electric. Cliff pushed close, his face twisted with anger and his fists clenched. "No way!" he said, softly. "You ain't puttin' nothin' in my room! And you ain't sleepin' there, either!"

"I was just doing what your dad told me to do," Ted protested.

Cliff pushed past and planted himself in the doorway to his room. "I don't care what the old man said. You ain't gettin' past me! Try it and you'll wish you'd paid attention to what I'm tellin' you!"

Ted shrugged and set down his suitcase. "OK," he said, "I'll just put my things out here in the hall."

Cliff nodded, triumph chasing the fury from his face. "Now you're bein' smart, Little Brother," he muttered. "You're bein' real smart. Keep that up and we'll get along OK."

Ted went back downstairs and out to the truck, his nervousness growing. He wanted to stop and tell Anne what had happened. He had been right about Cliff all along!

"Did Cliff show you where to put your things?" Mr. Denholm asked when Ted reached the half-empty truck.

Ted nodded. "Yeah, out in the hall."

Wilber Denholm stopped what he was doing. "What did you say?"

"Cliff doesn't like the idea of my bunking in with him, so I set my things in the hall."

The corners of Mr. Denholm's mouth tightened and, for an instant or two, deep concern flecked his mild eyes. "Cliff and I talked it over. I thought he understood that having the two of you share a room is the only thing we can do right now." He sighed deeply. "I'll go talk to him, Ted. You wait down here."

A few minutes later the other boy shuffled out the door, looking uneasy. "Ted?" he called.

Ted looked up, and for an instant he wanted to turn and leave, but he knew he couldn't.

"Ted?" Cliff repeated.

"Yeah?" Ted answered.

"I—I—" Cliff swallowed his words and began again. "I—I'm sorry about givin' you a bad time. I—I moved your stuff into my room. Th-that's where you'll be staying until we can figure some way to have a room for each of us."

Ted nodded. "Thanks." He wanted to add that he wasn't any more anxious to share the room than Cliff was to have him, but there was nothing he could do about it. However, this didn't seem to be the time to say any more.

Ted thought that was the end of the matter, but later in the afternoon, when the entire truck was unloaded and most things were unpacked, he went up to the room he and Cliff would be sharing. Cliff followed, closing the door behind them.

"I hope you're satisfied!" he growled. "You tried to get me in trouble with the old man!"

Ted turned to the window to hide his own anger. What Cliff said was true. He had chosen his words in a way that would let Mr. Denholm know, without saying so, exactly how he felt about Cliff shoving him around.

"Your dad asked me if I had my stuff moved in," he explained, "and I told him where it was. I wasn't going to lie about it."

"You did your best to get me in trouble, but it didn't work. The old man said I only had to have you in here with me until he can figure out something else. He'll probably put you out in the granary or the hay-mow!" He laughed loudly.

Ted turned and looked Cliff in the eye. "Just leave me alone. OK?"

Cliff went over to the dresser, picked up Ted's Bible, then tossed it back on the polished wood, as though the Bible meant nothing to him.

"I've got to put up with you in my room for awhile," he said, finally, "but I don't have to like it."

"And I have to put up with you too," Ted reminded him, "and I don't like it any better than you do."

Cliff snorted. "Watch it, Little Brother, or I'll forget what the old man said and mash that pretty face of yours."

Ted just glared back at Cliff.

Cliff moved closer. "Like I said, I have to put up with you, but I'm warnin' you! If you get your dirty little mitts on anything that belongs to me, I'll smear you." With that he whirled on his heel and went downstairs.

Ted Wills remained motionless in the center of the room, working his hands, one against the other. *Of all the guys in school, Cliff Denholm had to be the son of the man my mother married. Why couldn't it have been someone like Bart or Loren or Dave? Anybody else in the entire school, except Cliff Denholm. It just isn't fair!*

The following morning at breakfast, Mr. Denholm got his Bible and opened it to the Book of Romans.

"This is where we've been reading every morning," he explained, "so we'll continue with chapter 12." Slowly, carefully, he read the entire chapter. When he finished, he explained that they also knelt to pray.

"This is the way my father did it," he said. "And this is the way I hope each of you will pray when you're married and have families of your own—"

Ted looked quickly at Cliff and saw the smirk on his face. It was just as he thought. Cliff had no use for Christ.

They closed their eyes and Mr. Denholm began to pray. Ted had never heard anyone pray so sincerely, so earnestly. It seemed to him that he had never been as close to the Lord, except when he received Christ as his Saviour three or four years before.

It was Anita's turn next. She thanked God for her new mother. The tone of sincerity in her voice pleased Ted and he was sure it pleased his mother too. Then she thanked God for Anne and Ted. She asked Him to bring them all closer to God and closer to each other. After that she prayed for her dad and for Cliff and herself.

"—And make us a true family," she concluded. "In Jesus' name."

A long, taut silence followed. Ted wondered if Cliff would also pray. The pause continued for two or three minutes before the Denholm boy stumbled over a few mumbled words. Anne, who was kneeling across from Ted, prayed quickly. And so did he.

In a few minutes the time of prayer was over and they were on their feet again. As they rode to church that morning, all Ted could think of was their morning devotions. It was wonderful even to know a man like Mr. Denholm.

Sunday School that morning wasn't as bad as Ted had thought it might be. After a few songs and a Bible drill, everyone went to classes where nobody mentioned the fact that Mr. Denholm and Mrs. Wills had been married a few days before. At the morning service, however, the minister made up for any oversight.

Mr. Denholm and Ted's mom had insisted that they all sit together in a single pew, for one thing. For another, Pastor Fletcher called specific attention to them, saying that he had married the couple earlier in the week. Then, in his prayer, he asked God to bless the union of the two families. Ted felt like scooting to the floor and crawling out on his hands and knees.

Out of the corner of his eye, he saw that Cliff looked pale, and his lower lip was quivering. Anita, though, acted as if she were as happy as the boys were embarrassed. She reached over and squeezed her new mother's hand, possessively. Ted didn't mind that. He didn't think he would mind anything she did.

He thought his mom and Mr. Denholm would be upset by what the minister said. But if they were, they certainly did a good job of hiding it. They sat there, smiling, and when the service was over, everybody crowded around, congratulating them. They even seemed to enjoy that.

Ted had been wondering about the basketball goal and where they could put it up. However, he wasn't able to bring himself to ask Mr. Denholm about it until they were on their way home from church.

His new stepfather shook his head. "I'm sorry, I haven't given any thought to where we could put it," he answered, "but I'll tell you what we'll do. When dinner's over, you and Cliff and I will go out and see if we can find a good place for it. All right?"

That was fine with Ted, except that he wasn't sure about including Cliff. If it were anybody else—anybody who treated him decently, he wouldn't care, but having Cliff think he owned the goal could really cause trouble.

The family still seemed to feel self-conscious, eating Sunday dinner together. Quick bursts of conversation were separated by long periods of silence. Anita told of something that had happened in her Sunday School class, and everyone laughed as if it were the funniest thing they had ever heard.

They sat at the table longer than usual. No one seemed to know how to break away. Finally Cliff turned to his father. "Hey, Dad," he said, "isn't it about time for us to go out and find a place to put up our basketball goal?"

Ted glanced quickly at him. *Our* goal! Where did he get that *our* stuff? That goal was *his*! He'd earned every cent of the money to pay for it.

"Why don't you and Ted get your coats?" Mr. Denholm said. "I think I've got just the place for it, but I want to see what you guys think about it first."

Ted went up to get his coat, and Cliff was half a step behind him on the stairs. "Man," he said, almost civilly, "I hope it doesn't turn cold tonight like the radio says it's going to. I can hardly wait until we get our basketball goal up."

The Rangers
3 Make Plans

THE FOLLOWING MORNING, Cliff went to the frosted window as soon as he got up. He groaned aloud. "Just what I was afraid of!" he said.

Ted, who was still in bed, rolled over on one side and raised himself on one elbow. "Snow?"

"Nope. But the wind's blowin' like fury and, like the old man says, it looks cold enough out there to freeze the ears off a frog. We're not goin' to be able to put up our goal today."

"My goal!" Ted reminded him.

Cliff glanced quickly in his direction. "Your *goal!* But I get to use it!"

Ted didn't object to that. What bothered him was that his stepbrother hadn't asked. He had simply told Ted he was going to be out there shooting baskets whenever he wanted to. And he had said it in such a way that Ted knew he'd have trouble if he tried to stop Cliff.

Ted tried to change the subject, but Cliff was so excited about being able to play basketball at the farm that he kept right on talking. And for the moment, he seemed like a different guy.

"I'm sure glad you've got that goal," he said, shivering as he slid into his school clothes. "Basketball's my sport. You can have football and baseball."

He sat on the side of the bed and pulled on his shoes. "I've been tryin' and tryin' to get the old man to put up a goal and buy me a basketball so I can practice." He stood as though he was about to go downstairs. Instead, he turned back to Ted. "I'm goin' to try out for the team when I get to high school so I've got to have a place to practice."

Ted froze inside. It sounded to him as if Cliff was going to take over his basketball and goal. If he wasn't careful, he might not have either of them when he wanted them. And that wasn't fair. He had worked hard to earn all the money his stuff cost, and he had done it alone.

When the four young people left for school that morning after breakfast, it was obvious to Ted too, that they wouldn't be putting up a bastketball goal that day. The temperature had dropped to zero or below during the night. As the sun began to come up, the wind rose. It swept out of the northwest, driving the chill through their heavy coats and overshoes and mittens.

They left the farmyard and hurried down the lane to the road that led to town. It was early. The sun was still low in the eastern sky, but they had a three-mile walk, which took time.

Ted thought perhaps Mr. Denholm would get out

his car and take them, but he didn't. In fact he seemed to pay no attention to the fact that they were leaving. Instead, he went out to his machine shed to repair his tractor before time to use it in the spring.

They got to school a few minutes before the tardy bell. Ted was just coming in the front door when Bart and Dave came up to him.

"Hey," Bart exclaimed, "where've you been? We've been lookin' all over for you."

"What's up?" Ted asked.

"We've got to have a meeting of the Rangers," Dave said.

The decisive tone in his friend's voice disturbed him. "We've just had a meeting," Ted reminded them.

"We know." Bart lowered his voice to a hoarse whisper. "But we've got to have another one—tonight!"

Ted frowned. "How come?"

"S-s-sh!" Dave held a finger to his lips. "You know what a good detective says: 'Even the walls have ears.'"

"So," Bart added, "we decided we have to have a meeting of the Rangers tonight after school at our secret meeting place. OK?"

"I'm the president," Ted reminded them. "I call the meetings, and I can't have one tonight."

Bart frowned and said, "Why not?"

"I just can't make it. We have to walk home and Mom says we've got to walk together. Besides, only the president can call a meeting and I haven't done that."

They were deeply disturbed and showed it. "Where

does it say you've got to call the meetings?" Bart demanded. "Answer me that. It isn't in our bylaws."

"That's the way it is in all organizations," Ted bluffed. He didn't know for sure whether that was true or not, but it seemed as if he had heard it somewhere. At least that was the way it ought to be, and that was the way it was going to be in the Rangers.

"Can't you tell your mom about the meeting?" Bart asked. "It's important for you to be there."

Ted shook his head. "No way. But, maybe we could meet at noon. How about that?"

"The rest of us go home for dinner," Loren said.

"You could come back a little early," Ted suggested.

They discussed that possibility for a moment or two and decided it would work. "OK." We'll all come back early," Bart replied.

Ted gave the secret sign and the secret handshake and they hurried to their homeroom only seconds before the tardy bell rang.

The morning dragged endlessly for Ted. Even arithmetic, his favorite subject, didn't keep him from thinking about his hurried conversation with his friends. The Rangers had just had a meeting a few days before, taking care of all the business he knew about. He couldn't figure out why they should need another one so soon. Something awfully important must have come up.

Could they be testing him to see whether his moving to the farm had changed things? They might be dissatisfied with him as president, now that he lived out of town. Maybe they planned to elect one of the others to that important position. But they hadn't acted as though anything was wrong between themselves and him. Still, he couldn't be sure.

He glanced uneasily at the clock on the wall behind Miss Winslow's desk. It was 11:35. It wouldn't be long until he would know what was going on. Finally the bell rang, releasing them for an hour at noon.

It was easy to know which kids lived close enough to their homes so they could walk home. They clattered noisily to the coat racks and charged out into the cold November air.

Those who were eating at school were a little slower to move. They let the surge of town kids pass, then went for their lunch pails. They'd eat their lunches in their homerooms if the weather was cold. If it was warm out, they'd sit on the front steps of the building and play games afterward.

Ted hadn't realized what he and Anne had missed by going home for dinner. On that particular day, however, he wasn't thinking about the fun he would have when they finished eating. He was watching for the Rangers so they could have their meeting.

By this time, Ted was sure that only a serious problem would get them to go over his head and call a special meeting. They hadn't done that before. He was sure they were going to replace him as president. They might even ask him to resign from the club.

But he was wrong.

They met in one corner of the long hall a few moments before the bell called them to their afternoon classes. "My dad's in the Commercial Club," Bart said, guardedly, when they were all together.

Ted nodded. He knew that Mr. Harrison operated one of the local service stations and took an active part in town affairs.

"Well, he was telling me last night that the Commercial Club is going to sponsor a junior basketball league this winter."

Ted eyed Bart and Dave, blankly. He couldn't figure out what that would have to do with the Rangers, and said so.

"Didn't I tell you? Dad's going to sponsor a team and be one of the coaches. He said the Rangers can be his team, if we want to!"

Ted's eyes brightened momentarily. "If we want to?" he exclaimed. "Man, we'd have to be off our rockers to turn down a deal like that."

"That's exactly what we said," Loren added.

And then a thought rushed in to chill him. He eyed Bart questioningly. "Of course I'm still the president!" he said, firmly.

Bart nodded. "Having Dad sponsor us as his basketball team wouldn't change that."

"I just wanted to be sure we understand each other," Ted said. "I'm the president and *I* decide about such things."

He saw his friends stiffen.

"*We* decide those things!" Dave declared. "Remember, we all have a vote!"

"I know, but the president is the boss," Ted said.

"We'll have to see about that!" Dave replied.

Ted realized he had gone too far and backed off slightly. "Of course we usually all want to do the same things," he said, "so it doesn't make any difference—I happen to feel the same as you do about the basketball team, Bart. It's great!"

That seemed to relieve the tension. At least no one challenged him further.

"That's what we thought," Bart said. He pulled in a deep breath. "Only we do have a little problem."

"Like what?" Ted asked.

"We've got to come up with two or three more guys. We need five regulars and one sub."

"They don't have to be in the Rangers, do they?" Ted said.

"That's something we'll have to decide," Bart told him.

"Well," Ted answered decisively, "I don't think they should. We start taking in guys and the first thing we know, we'll lose control of it. The club, I mean."

He didn't like the idea, but they all insisted on voting on it. Dave was in favor of letting the new guys join the Rangers. But fortunately, Bart and Loren felt the same as Ted did. They voted to take new guys on the basketball team but not to let them be club members.

"Now," Ted continued, "I've got to decide who we're going to ask to play with us."

"*We* have to decide," Dave reminded him coldly.

"That's right," Bart said. "We all vote on this."

He didn't challenge them, but he was surprised at their first suggestion. "I think that new brother of yours would be super," Dave said. "He's the best basketball player in sixth grade."

"New brother?" Ted echoed. He knew who Dave meant and his face flushed. "I don't have any new brother."

"Sure you do," Dave said, "Cliff Denholm."

"We may live at the same house," Ted blurted, irritably, "but he's no brother of mine."

"Dave's right," Bart put in. "Cliff's plenty good. I think we ought to grab him before somebody else does."

"He's good, all right," Loren observed. "I remember last year when he made 16 free throws without a miss."

"And he's big," Dave added. "He's taller than any of us. Think you can talk him into playing with our team?"

Ted frowned, looking from one to the other, uncertainly. The trouble was that the other guys didn't really know Cliff like he did. They knew he was pushy but not how bad he was. After a week he'd be ordering everybody around—especially Ted. "Are you guys sure you really want him?"

"Why wouldn't we?" Loren persisted. "He's good. He's awful good."

Ted hesitated. It was no use in arguing that Cliff couldn't play well enough to make the team. Everybody knew how good he was. He had to have some other reason for keeping his stepbrother off the Ranger's team. "He's a *different* guy when you really get to know him," he said.

"I don't think he's so bad," Loren said. "I used to run around with him a little before his mom died." He paused. "I kinda like the guy."

They were all looking at Ted. "What do you think?"

"If I was doing it—I'd find somebody else. We don't want to pick the first guy we think of."

Dave took his jackknife from his pocket and fingered it. "I still think Cliff's the best guy we could find for center."

Ted flushed with anger as he leaned forward intently. "If you want him to play with the Rangers, OK. Go ahead and ask him. But don't say I didn't warn you."

He didn't call for a vote on having Cliff play with their team but brought up the names of a couple of other guys. Loren mentioned someone and Bart had two more friends he thought they could get.

"OK, let's take a vote," Ted said.

Bart got a piece of notebook paper, tore it up, and they voted secretly. When the ballots were counted, Ted was relieved to learn that they had settled on two other fellows.

Ted didn't say anything to anyone, especially Cliff, about the basketball league. He soon learned, however, that it was the worst kept secret in school. They hadn't left the school yard before Cliff started telling him about it. "You and I ought to get up a team, Ted," he said. "We could find some other guys and have a great time. We'd win some games with a goal out on the farm to use for practice."

Ted glanced warily at him. Did Cliff know about

the Rangers' team? Was he trying to get Ted to ask him to play with them? "Sorry, but I'm going to be playing with Bart Harrison. His dad's our coach."

Cliff's eyes gleamed and Ted realized this was the first he had known about the Rangers' team. "S'pose Mr. Harrison needs another guy?" he asked. "I'd sure like to play with you."

He shook his head. "I don't think there's room for anyone else. I'm sure they've got everybody they need." He hoped no one would tell about his trying to keep Cliff off their team. He would get in trouble if his mom and Anne and Mr. Denholm found out.

Cliff's eyes narrowed and he looked as if he were about to say something.

Ted turned away, deliberately, and Cliff said no more until they got back to the farm. Mr. Denholm had started the chores. He had told Ted's mother to send the boys out to the barn to help him.

"But you'd better change your clothes first," she said.

Sudden anger flecked Cliff's eyes. "*Yes, Ma'am*," he muttered. "Right away, *Ma'am*."

Ted felt like challenging Cliff. He didn't like to hear him talk to his mom like that. But saying something to Cliff would only make things worse. And then his mom would get after him.

The fact that it was cold and disagreeable only increased the work load. They had to throw down hay for the cows and mules then break the ice on the water in the tank so the animals could drink. The pigs and chickens had to be fed, and the corral gate had to be repaired. It was after dark when they finally finished and were able to go into the house and drop, wearily, into chairs at the kitchen table.

"You're learning fast, Ted," Mr. Denholm said. "You're a big help already."

Cliff's head came up, a knowing grin tugging at one corner of his mouth. "Yeah, he's finally reached the place where he can almost feed the calves without gettin' himself killed."

Mr. Denholm scowled. "Cliff," he said, mildly. "That's not very nice."

Ted's face got red and he felt himself getting angry.

After supper Anita got her notebook and came to Ted. "You said you were good at arithmetic, didn't you, Ted?"

"Him?" her brother broke in quickly. "Don't make me laugh! All he's good at is settin' in church."

"Cliff!" Mr. Denholm exclaimed.

"Well, it's the truth," Cliff said.

"Would you help me?" Anita repeated.

"Sure, 'Nita." Ignoring her brother, Ted scooted around in his chair so he could look at her paper. "What's the problem?"

"I just don't understand any of it," she said.

Cliff shouldered in, roughly. "Here, I'll help you."

"The last time you helped me, I had them all wrong," she told Cliff.

He turned away, muttering to himself.

Later, they all sat around the table, listening to the radio. Cliff began to boast about being in the all-school chautauqua again next spring. "That'll make three years in a row for me," he announced.

"How do you know you're going to make it again?" Anita asked. "They'll be having tryouts like always. You might not make it this time."

He drew himself up and looked haughtily from one to the other. "I've made it the last two years, haven't I?" He breathed deeply. "Actually, I've made it every year I've tried. They don't have another magician in the whole school who dares try out against me."

"Maybe you haven't had competition before," Anne retorted, "but you do now."

Cliff looked surprised, and Ted certainly was. He was sure his sister meant him, and he was amazed that she would speak up for him.

"If there's anybody in Elmville who has nerve enough to come up against me, I don't know about it," Cliff said, a little nervously.

"This person has been at it long enough to be very good," Anne said quietly.

Cliff snorted. "That, I'd have to see."

"I'm not an expert," Anne continued, "but I've seen him perform lots of times and he's good!"

Ted frowned at her. He wished she'd be quiet. He didn't feel like getting into a contest with his stepbrother.

"Just who is this so-called magician?" Cliff persisted.

Anne turned to Ted, and he saw that she was pale and wheezing slightly from the confrontation. "Ted," she said, "why don't you show Cliff one of your tricks?"

Cliff gasped. "You?"

Ted grimaced.

"You do magic tricks?" Cliff said. "That's a laugh."

"C'mon, Ted," Anne begged. "Show him."

"I don't feel like it right now," Ted replied.

"Come on," Cliff jeered. "If you're as good as all that, show us what you can do." He laughed. "Maybe I can learn a few things."

"Yes," Mr. Denholm added. "Show us a couple of tricks, Ted. We'd like to see them."

Reluctantly, Ted got to his feet. "What should I do?" he asked Anne, though he didn't really want to talk to her. He felt more like kicking her in the shins.

"How about the disappearing bird cage?" she suggested.

"The disappearing bird cage!" Cliff exclaimed, amazement widening his eyes. "You've got to be kidding! You can't do that one."

"I told you he was good!" Anne exclaimed. "And that's not the only trick he's got. He has a huge box filled with them."

"You're puttin' me on!" Cliff retorted.

"Just wait and see," Anne said.

The color left Cliff's face, and he moved back from the table. "I've got some studying to do. I haven't got all night to waste sitting around here."

Anne looked pleased as the stairway door closed behind him.

Ted felt shaken. It was so unlike Anne to pick a fight, especially with someone besides him. Yet the more he thought about it, the more pleased he was. He knew now that Cliff's bragging had finally gotten to her too.

Basket-
4ball Begins

MR. DENHOLM had promised Cliff that he would fix another room so he could be alone. But two weeks passed before he bought the material and started remodeling the sewing room on the main floor. In a few days, it was ready. It was smaller than the upstairs room but had the advantage of being closer to the heating stove in the living room; so Cliff, who got his choice, moved into it.

That didn't bother Ted. He was used to sleeping upstairs in the cold and was glad to have a room to himself. That way he didn't have to worry about Cliff trying to get into his box of magic. He checked the padlock periodically. Once he suspected it had been tampered with, but he couldn't be sure so he didn't say anything about it.

He hoped to get his basketball goal up so he could start practicing. But the temperature stayed unusually low for November, and some powdery snows fell too.

The guys at school all knew about the new junior basketball league long before the formal announcement was made. There were rumors about who was going to have teams and which guys were going to play where. But no final decisions were officially made until the rules were published. Both the names and sponsors of the teams were announced. Cliff read the account with great interest.

"Sid Crawford was supposed to play with you guys, wasn't he?" Cliff asked.

Ted nodded uneasily. It sounded as if Cliff was leading up to something, so he began to move toward the stairway door to go to his room. However, Cliff would not let him go.

"I was talkin' to Sid today," Cliff continued. "I guess his old man's goin' to have a team, so he'll be playin' with them."

Ted's heart sank. He knew what was coming next.

"That means you'll need another guy on the Rangers' team, doesn't it?" Cliff demanded, his gaze fixed intently on Ted.

"I don't know for sure," Ted answered lamely. "Bart or his dad may have already found somebody."

"They couldn't have," Cliff replied, his eyes gleaming triumphantly. "I asked Sid not to tell Bart about it until tomorrow afternoon. That'll give you time to talk to Bart about my playing in Sid's place."

Ted didn't reply.

"You will talk to him, won't you?" he demanded, suspiciously.

"The guys will have to vote on it," Ted said.

"Now, listen!" Cliff retorted, angrily. "You're the president of the Rangers."

Ted looked at him hard. "Who told you that?" he demanded.

"It's true isn't it?" Cliff said.

Ted hesitated. That was supposed to be one of the club's best kept secrets. He hadn't even told Anne or his mother. He didn't know how Cliff could possibly have found out. "Who said that?"

"It's true. Don't try to act as if it isn't," Cliff went on. "And I can tell you something else. You can get the other guys to vote for me, if you want to."

"They'll have to vote first. I can't promise you anything. Why don't you play with Sid's team? They won't have their guys yet."

"I already talked to Sid," Cliff said. "His dad's going to pick the guys, and Sid didn't think they'd need me."

Ted saw just a touch of desperation in Cliff's face. He felt mean, but added, "What about the drugstore team? You know Mr. Arnold. Why don't you ask him to let you play?"

"I already have." This time discouragement was heavy in Cliff's voice. "They don't need me either."

That ought to tell him something, Ted thought to himself. *People would rather have a guy who got along with everyone and didn't play as well.*

"You'll talk to them, won't you?" Cliff said again.

"I'll see what they want to do," Ted agreed.

"Great. You keep that up and you and me'll get along fine," Cliff said with his usual swagger.

"But I can't promise anything," Ted warned.

Cliff's lips tightened and his voice lowered. "Listen,

don't give me that stuff. I know you can get me on the team if you want to."

"We all have a vote," Ted said again. "If you get enough votes, you're in."

Cliff leaned closer. "And if I don't, I'm out. Is that it?" The words wore a knife edge.

Ted nodded.

"If you get me on your team, I won't tell anybody you're the president of the Rangers," Cliff continued. "But if you don't, word's goin' to spread all over school. That's a promise." He stuck out his chin. "And that's just the beginning! If you know what's good for you, you'll see that they vote for me."

Ted exploded. "If that's the way you feel about it, go ahead and tell anything you please. You can just forget about playing with the Rangers." He drew himself erect. "To tell you the truth, I don't think they'd want you on the team, anyway."

Cliff's neck flushed and he managed a weak grin. "Forget what I just said. I was only kidding. You ought to know I wouldn't do anything to you— After all, we're practically in the same family. You're my stepbrother."

Ted really hadn't wanted to talk to the other guys about Cliff playing with the Rangers. Somebody had already brought up Cliff's name and the guys had decided against him. If it came up again, Dave and the others might think he had changed his mind and actually wanted Cliff to play with them. Still, he had promised.

The guys had already heard about Sid Crawford

leaving the Rangers' team to play with the quintet his dad was sponsoring. However, they hadn't yet made a decision about a replacement. Ted mentioned Cliff's name, carelessly, during the discussion, as though he weren't really all that serious. However, the others sounded as though they would actually consider having Cliff on the team.

"He's a lot better than Sid ever thought of being," Dave said. "He's fast and a real deadeye when it comes to the basket."

Loren nodded. "And he's taller than any of us. He'd be perfect for center."

Ted felt the muscles in his stomach tighten. He hadn't expected that. The guys were serious about having Cliff. And that was the last thing he wanted. Finally they read the disapproval in his eyes and asked what he thought about it.

Ted shrugged indifferently. "He can play basketball OK, but there's something I think we ought to ask ourselves. Not one other team has asked him to play with them. Why haven't they? Have you ever thought about that?"

They shook their heads.

"As good as he is," Ted continued, "why do you suppose no one else has picked him?"

Only one voted for Cliff, and that wasn't Ted. But he was the one who had to tell his stepbrother about the vote.

"Thanks," Cliff muttered when Ted told him. "Thanks a lot." He turned away quickly, his face dark with anger.

"It wasn't my fault," Ted called after him. "I told you from the start that it might happen."

Cliff reached the door before turning back, belligerence in every move. "I know what you told me," he grated. "And I know I didn't have a chance of getting to play, with you running the meeting. You torpedoed me. I hope you got what you wanted."

Ted cringed. He really hadn't told the guys to vote against Cliff. They'd made that decision on their own, but he had let them know how he felt about it. His sleep was troubled that night. Still, he knew what it would have been like if they had allowed Cliff to play with them. Before they had even started playing, he would have been trying to run everything. And the guys wouldn't have liked that.

Although the players for all the teams were selected and had started practicing, the first games were to be played when classes resumed after Christmas vacation. Cliff said no more to Ted about not getting to play with the Rangers, or the fact that no other team had asked him to play with them. In fact, he acted as though it didn't matter. But when the schedule was announced and he saw that the games were to be played on Saturday mornings, he was furious.

"It isn't fair!" he exploded at home. "There's nothing fair about it!" He shouted so loudly everyone could hear him.

"Keep your voice down, Cliff," his dad said quietly. "We're sitting right here in the living room."

"I can't help it, Dad!" He sounded as if he were close to tears. "Since Ted came out here to live, I don't get a fair shake around here. He's going to be playin' basketball every Saturday morning. That means I'll have all the work to do."

His dad laid aside the magazine he had been reading. "There isn't that much work at this time of year, and the basketball season will be over before the spring work starts."

"That's what you say because it's Ted playin' basketball," Cliff accused. "If it was me, you'd be tellin' me that I couldn't play. I'd have to work."

Mr. Denholm shook his head. "As a matter of fact, Cliff," he said, "you can play basketball Saturday mornings, too, if you want to."

For a brief instant the boy hesitated, his lips quivering. "You're just sayin' that because of Ted! You can let him play basketball all you want to, but I'm not leavin' you alone with the work."

Ted squirmed uneasily as Cliff stormed through the kitchen to the back porch where he jerked on his heavy coat and overshoes. Ted supposed this was going to ruin his chance of getting to go into town to play basketball. He talked with his mother about it.

"Why don't you ask Dad?" she suggested.

Mr. Denholm surprised him by insisting he play. Ted should have felt good about it, but he didn't. Mr. Denholm might not know why Cliff felt the way he did, but Ted knew. And he knew who was responsible!

The Ruined 5 Ball

FOR A WEEK, the temperature stayed near zero. The north wind was sharp and cutting. It had swept the snow from the farmyard and the road to town, and piled it in great drifts along the fencerows.

Walking to school was an ordeal. When the kids finally got to town, their cheeks and noses were stung to a cherry red and their feet ached. Ted's fingers were so stiff with the cold that he dropped his books as he shifted them from one hand to the other in order to open the school door. Anita helped him pick up his things, and they walked down the hall together, enjoying the warmth of the building.

"I wish they'd build a hall like this all the way out to our place," Ted said. "Then walking home wouldn't be so bad."

"But it seems so good to get inside again after being out in the cold," she said, laughing. "Now that I'm used to it, I sort of like it."

He didn't know whether he agreed with her or not. It was on days like this that he wished they still lived in town, so they wouldn't have so far to walk in the bitter cold.

Anne caught cold during the severe weather; the cold turned into a bad asthma attack. They had to have the doctor come out for her. He prescribed bed rest and gave her some green powder to burn called *Asthmador*. "The smoke will help her breathe," he explained.

Ted didn't like the sharp smell of the powder burning, but he and Anita sat in Anne's room with her as much as they could. Cliff, however, showed no concern for Anne. Ted wondered if he was holding a grudge because she had spoken up that day about his magic act.

When Anne was finally able to return to school, Mr. Denholm took them all so she wouldn't have to walk and risk catching cold again.

Relief from the bitter weather came suddenly— overnight in early December. They all went to bed, fighting off the chill, and woke up the next morning to see little puddles of melted snow scattered across the yard. The temperature was a pleasant 40° F. Ted could hardly believe it.

When he went downstairs, Cliff was in the living room, pulling on his boots and lacing them. Ted went over to the window. "Hey, man!" he exclaimed to Cliff. "Look out there, would you? We've got a spring day!"

Cliff grunted and laced his other boot. "So what? It'll just turn cold again."

"Maybe so." Ted was about to mention that it might

be a good time to put up his basketball goal, then decided not to. "But I'm goin' to enjoy this while we've got it."

Ted intended to get Mr. Denholm alone sometime later, maybe that night, and talk to him about putting it up, but he didn't have to. Mr. Denholm mentioned it himself while they were eating breakfast. Cliff glared at his father. "Why're you goin' to waste time doin' that?"

"For one thing," his father said, "I promised Ted we'd put it up as soon as it got warm enough. For another, I thought you two would enjoy shooting a few baskets."

Cliff pushed back from the table. "Maybe Ted will, but I won't. I haven't got time for that kid stuff!"

Ted didn't know whether to be pleased or unhappy with Cliff's attitude. It sounded as if his stepbrother wouldn't want to shoot baskets at all. That meant he wouldn't have to worry about Cliff taking over. On the other hand, it wasn't nearly as much fun shooting baskets alone as it was with someone else.

The wind came up during the day, and Ted was afraid it might turn cold again before they got home. However, it was still warm in the late afternoon, and Mr. Denholm was waiting. He had his tools and some bolts ready, and the ladder was leaning against the building.

It didn't take long for the two of them to secure the basket on the front of the granary, a regulation 10 feet from the rim of the hoop to the ground. Ted help the hoop in place while Mr. Denholm tightened the lock-washer nuts. They were just finishing when Cliff came up.

"You're a little late to help us put up the goal," his dad said, "but I guess you're not too late to help Ted try it out."

Cliff kicked a cob over the thawing ground. "It's Ted's goal," he said, bitterly. "You've never bought anything like that for me, but Ted comes out here to live and what happens? Right away you get him a basketball goal."

"That isn't true, Cliff. Ted already had the goal. And he worked to save money to buy it himself."

"Well, you're helping him put it up," Cliff retorted.

"I'd do the same for you or Anita or Anne," his dad said.

"It makes me sick to see how things are goin' around here now! Nothing's like it was!" Cliff grumbled. He spun on his heel and strode off.

The weather was mild for a couple of days, so Ted shot baskets every chance he had. The first day, Cliff ignored him, but then he began to pester Ted. Cliff would deliberately stand where he could get the rebound. Then he'd keep the ball from Ted, holding it high enough or far enough away so shorter Ted couldn't reach it.

"Come on!" Ted exclaimed, exasperated and almost worn out from trying to get the ball away from the bigger, stronger boy. "Let's have it!"

"I'm trainin' you!" Cliff taunted. "Come on, show me how good you are! Take the ball away from me!"

Ted lunged angrily for it, but Cliff was taller and

faster. He flicked the ball just beyond Ted's reach.

"Give it to me!" Ted cried.

"Beg!" Cliff said as he held the ball high and fended Ted off with his other hand. "That's it, Fido. Beg!"

Wilber Denholm came around the corner of the granary just then. "Cliff!" he exclaimed, sternly. "What's going on here?"

His son backed away sheepishly, and tossed the ball to Ted. "We—we were just havin' a little fun, that's all."

"It doesn't look like fun to me," Mr. Denholm said. "I won't have anymore of that, do you hear?"

Cliff muttered something under his breath and turned away until his father went out to the shop where he was working at his forge. As soon as he was out of sight, Cliff came back and snatched the ball from Ted again.

"Give it to me," Ted demanded.

"What're you goin' to do, Little Brother? Tell the old man on me?"

"Give it to me," Ted repeated.

"Why don't you use some of your great magic?" Cliff taunted. "Make the ball fly out of my hands to yours, if you're so good."

"I'm better than you are," Ted declared.

"That I'll have to see!" Cliff said.

Again, Ted grabbed for the ball, but his stepbrother jerked it from him, running quickly backward. When Cliff was half a dozen paces away, he drew back his arm and fired the ball past Ted, slamming it into the side of the granary.

The ball immediately deflated. Ted walked over and picked it up. It must have hit a nail. It was badly torn. A heavier, more expensive ball might have survived, but this one was ruined.

Ted groaned. "Look what you've done!"

Cliff stared at it, and a flicker of concern crossed his face. Then he stiffened and growled, "Go ahead! Tell the old man on me. See if I care!"

Ted didn't answer. The ball was ruined, and he'd hardly had a chance to use it. What's more he didn't have the money to buy a new one and no way of earning any. Now that they lived in the country, he couldn't even gather up pop bottles and earn a few cents that way.

He shuffled into the house, the ruined ball under his arm. Though hurt and angry, he decided not to say anything to anyone about it. So he was surprised when Anita got him in the living room alone after supper and spoke to him about it.

"It was just one of those things," he said, disappointment thick in his voice. "How did you know about it?"

"I saw the whole thing. I was out in the yard," she told him. "My brother can be so mean sometimes. But I don't think he meant to ruin your ball."

"He could have fooled me," Ted said bitterly.

"Are you going to tell Dad?" she asked.

He shrugged. "What good would that do?"

"He'll punish Cliff if you do," she said.

"Don't you think he deserves it?" he asked.

"I suppose so," she said, fighting back tears. "But

what he really needs is to receive Christ. That's his problem. He doesn't have the Lord Jesus to help him live the way he should."

Ted nodded.

"If you won't tell Dad, I—I'll help Cliff save money to buy you a new basketball." Her eyes pleaded with him. "It'll take us a while, but—"

"You don't have to help him get me a new ball, 'Nita," he said. "And you don't have to worry about my telling Dad."

Her eyes lit gratefully, and for one awful instant, he was afraid she was going to kiss him. He backed away uneasily.

"Thank you," she said, smiling. "You're one of the nicest brothers a girl could have."

He didn't tell her so, but he thought she was mighty nice too.

Anita stood there a minute, as though uncertain about something. Then she said, "Ted, I've been praying and praying that Cliff would receive Christ as his Saviour and live the way a Christian should." She laid a hand on his arm. "I know Dad's praying for him too. Would you join us?"

"Sure," he promised.

She touched his cheek quickly and again said, "Thank you."

That night the wind switched to the north and roared across the prairies, driving the temperatures down again. Winter was back, savagely.

Christmas was near, and the stores along Elmville's lone main street were bright with colored lights, balls, and tinsel. Most of the homes had lights around the doors or on an evergreen in the yard.

Even the Denholms had found money for a tree. To be sure, it was so scrawny the price had been marked down; but it was a Christmas tree and that was all that mattered. The family decorated it with lights, colored balls, and strings of popcorn and cranberries. When they finished, Ted thought it was the most beautiful tree he'd ever seen.

True to his promise, he had not told Mr. Denholm about the ball, but the older man noticed he wasn't shooting baskets and asked about it.

The color rose in Ted's cheeks. "Had a little hard luck," he said, explaining about the nail in the side of the granary. "I guess the ball's ruined."

Cliff squirmed uncomfortably, especially when his dad asked Ted to bring the ball down so he could look at it. Cliff would have left the table, but his dad stopped him.

"We're going to have devotions in a few minutes."

"Again?" Cliff demanded, scornfully. "We already had them this morning."

"We always have devotions twice a day before Thanksgiving, Christmas, and Easter. You know that, Cliff."

Ted handed the ball to Mr. Denholm while Cliff studied his plate nervously. Both he and Anita were watching Ted to see what he was going to say. Mr. Denholm examined the ball.

"I don't really think there's any use in looking at it," Ted said. "I'm sure it's ruined."

"Yeah, Ted," Cliff broke in, defensively. "You ought to be more careful."

Mr. Denholm agreed with Ted that the basketball was too badly torn to repair. When he finished examining it, he laid it on the floor beside him and opened his Bible.

Ted hoped he might get another basketball for Christmas. At first he made himself believe it could happen, but he realized he should have known better. Even though the ball he had bought himself wasn't expensive, Mom and Mr. Denholm didn't have money for that kind of gift.

They gave Cliff and Ted shirts and Anita and Anne blouses. As far as Ted could tell, they bought nothing for each other. And since the children had no money, they couldn't give anything to their parents either.

Still, it was a great holiday season. They went to church early Christmas Eve for the Sunday School program. Then they came home and sang carols with Mom at the piano. Afterward, Mr. Denholm read the Christmas story from the Bible. Then they opened their gifts, and ended the evening popping corn and making fudge.

The next day they would have roast chicken and dressing for dinner, with wedges of mincemeat pie. Yes, Ted told himself as he crawled into bed and closed his eyes to pray. This had been a great Christmas, even though he hadn't gotten the basketball he longed for.

Tournament
6 Play and
Old Blue

THE RANGERS' basketball team did well in the new league. They won their first three games quite easily but were nosed out by a single point in the fourth game after Ted fouled out midway in the second half. They dropped the next game by seven points and came surging back to win the last two games. That put them in the play-offs to decide the championship.

Cliff pretended not to be concerned about whether the Rangers won or lost, but he always seemed to have lots of advice for Ted after each contest. "You'd have knocked those guys off easy if I'd been playin'," he said after one game. "I'd have been good for at least 8 or 10 points more. That would have won the game in a walkaway. He paused and lowered his voice. "In fact, if I'd been playin', you'd have made a clean sweep so far. Not a team in the league could've stopped us. You made one big mistake by not lettin' me play with you."

Ted sipped his milk, thoughtfully. It would be great to be as good as Cliff said he was. When his stepbrother boasted that way, it was all Ted could do to keep from asking Cliff why, if he was such a star, none of the teams wanted him. But he decided to keep quiet. He didn't want to get into that hassle with Cliff again.

"You'll knock off the Westside Yanks without any trouble," Cliff prophesied. "And you might even beat the Terriers, if you get real lucky and don't have too many fouls. But watch out for the Smoke Eaters. They're gettin' better all the time."

"We'll do our best," Ted told him. "That's all anybody can do."

"Yeah," Cliff snickered. "I guess that's right. Of course, if *I* was playin' with you, it'd be different. We'd take 'em all."

"Cliff," Mr. Denholm said, looking up at his son. "Don't you think this bragging has gone on long enough?"

Something inside Cliff went off suddenly. "That's right!" he cried, his voice shaking with emotion. "Rip into me! I'm to blame for everything that goes wrong around here! I knew what it would be like when you got married again! Whatever happens, you have to protect that pet of yours! You're afraid *she'll* get mad if you don't!" He pointed at Ted's mother.

"That isn't true, Son." He would have gone on, but Cliff left the room abruptly and the rest of the family, stunned by the outburst, sat in silence.

It was only a moment or two until Cliff Denholm came out, ready to go out to the barn. "*I* have work on Saturday mornings! But, what's your little darling going to do? He'll be enjoying himself, playin' basketball!"

Mr. Denholm's eyes flashed and he said sternly, "Clifford, go to your room and wait there for me!"

The boy's defiance slackened. "I can't, Dad," he said, almost apologetically. "I've got to get out and milk."

"The cows will be there when we've finished talking. Now, *do as I say!*"

Ted didn't know what took place in Cliff's room, but Mr. Denholm and his son were there for a long time. When they finally returned to the kitchen, Cliff was subdued. He mumbled a pained apology to Ted and shuffled outside.

"I'm sorry for what he said, Ted," Mr. Denholm told his stepson when the other boy was gone. "He's all mixed up." Mr. Denholm poured himself another cup of coffee. "If only there was some way I could get through to him. I've tried reasoning with him and reassuring him. I've tried shaming him. I've tried disciplining him, but nothing seems to work." He sighed deeply. "I don't know what to do."

But that wasn't all that was troubling Wilber Denholm. Ted had noticed the change in his stepfather's morning prayers. He prayed longer and more earnestly about the weather than ever before.

So Ted began to talk to God about it too. However, he didn't say anything to his stepfather until one evening that week. He found Mr. Denholm in the barn, standing and looking at the cattle.

"Mr. Denholm," Ted began.

His stepfather didn't seem to hear him.

Ted came up beside him. "Mr. Denholm," he said again, louder this time.

The graying man turned and smiled thinly. Ted thought that he caught a tear glistening in the man's tired eyes. "Yes?"

"Is something wrong?" Ted asked.

"No," Mr. Denholm answered quickly. Then he stopped and a crooked smile lifted one corner of his mouth. "That's not true. Something is terribly wrong." Leaning against the manger, he told Ted about the serious lack of moisture and of his concern for their family, as well as the cattle and mules.

"A man should take care of his stock," he said. "That's one thing my father drilled into me. 'A man shouldn't have animals unless he takes care of them,' he'd say. But I don't have the money to buy hay. I've gotten by this winter with what we raised last year, but from now on—" He gestured helplessly. "How can I feed them the way I should unless it rains?"

"I've been praying for rain too," Ted said impulsively. "Now I'm going to pray harder than ever, *Dad*."

Mr. Denholm smiled and put an arm about his shoulder. "Thanks, Son."

For a long while they remained motionless.

"There's something else that I've been wanting to talk to you about, Ted. I guess this is about as good a time as any."

There was a long silence. "I know how ornery Cliff has been at times."

Ted didn't answer but did nod slightly.

"He took the death of his mother very hard. It was rough enough for all of us, but he was shaken more deeply than 'Nita or me."

"I know what he went through," Ted said.

"You would at that—" Mr. Denholm's voice grew distant. "When I began to see your mother, I tried to explain how I felt to both Cliff and 'Nita. She could understand that my going out with your mother had nothing to do with my loving their mother less. But Cliff couldn't—or wouldn't. As a result, this whole experience of my getting married and your moving out to the farm has been very hard for him."

Ted nodded. "Is—is there anything I can do to help?"

Mr. Denholm shrugged. "I don't—I really don't know. I guess I just hope you can understand why Cliff is behaving as he is."

"I—I'll try," Ted said.

"And, Ted," his stepfather said, smiling faintly. "Pray for Cliff, won't you?"

Ted gave his solemn promise.

*   *   *

Cliff had avoided speaking to Ted following his blowup. But after the second tournament game that Saturday, he broke his self-imposed silence.

"Well, you beat Westside," he said to Ted. "And now you've beaten the Terriers, just like I said you would."

"Actually, they didn't give us all that much trouble," Ted told him. "We got out in front toward the end of the first quarter and were never behind the rest of the game."

Cliff laughed scornfully. "I told you about that, and I also told you about playing the Smoke Eaters. They'll teach you Rangers a little basketball."

"They're good, all right," Ted agreed.

"You'll never see the day when you can even come close to holding them," Cliff said.

There was a brief silence.

"How about a little bet? Say a buck. I'll take the Smoke Eaters," Cliff suggested.

"I don't bet," Ted said.

"That's wise, Little Brother," Cliff said. "That's very wise. If I were in your place, I'd be against betting too. They're goin' to skin you! But good!" He walked away, laughing.

The following Saturday the Rangers met the Smoke Eaters for the championship. It was a hard-fought game from the opening whistle, with the lead changing half a dozen times a quarter. First the Smoke Eaters would forge ahead a couple of points. Then the Rangers would score to tie it up and make a free throw or two.

At halftime, they were tied and at the end of the third quarter the Smoke Eaters were ahead. Then Ted and his pals had a hot streak and stole the lead again. Once they got ahead in the fourth quarter, they hung on grimly, fighting off every rally their opponents tried to uncork. When the ending gun sounded, the Rangers had won by a scant three points.

The Rangers were presented with the trophy and

Ted, as president, insisted on taking it home first. Bart Harrison challenged him. "My dad sponsored the team. I get to have it first!"

"No way!" Pride and arrogance gleamed in Ted's eyes. "I'm the president! I get the trophy first."

"We'll take a vote on it!" Bart said.

"No vote! What I say goes!" Ted held the trophy tightly.

Mr. Harrison came up just then and settled the matter by taking the trophy to his service station to display for a couple of weeks. "Then it will go to you for two weeks, Ted," he said. "And after that the other guys will each get to keep it."

Ted couldn't say he liked the arrangement, but he could do nothing about it. Mr. Harrison had sponsored the team; so he had some rights when it came to deciding what happened to the trophy.

The rest of the Rangers accepted the sponsor's ruling, but for some reason they seemed angry with Ted. He couldn't understand why. It wasn't his fault that the Commercial Club hadn't provided a trophy for each of them.

As he left the Harrison basement for home, he realized he had left his jacket at the bottom of the stairs and went back for it. He was on his way the second time when he heard Dave say, "I get so disgusted with Ted Wills I can hardly stand it. He's sure got the big head."

Ted stopped suddenly and almost turned back. The guys didn't have any right to think such things about him.

All the way home he could think of little else. He didn't want the gang to think he was conceited. At first he thought he would try to straighten them out the first chance he had. Then he decided Dave was just jealous because Ted was going to be the first of the guys to take the trophy home and keep it for two weeks. After all, that was the president's privilege. If he didn't get to do things like that, what was the advantage of being president?

Mr. Denholm asked Ted and Cliff to harness up the mules that afternoon as soon as the boys finished lunch.

"I'd be helping you myself," he said, "but Mom and I have to go to town this afternoon. The way the dirt's beginning to blow, I figure we've got to start harrowing and stop as much of it as we can."

Ted waited for Cliff to reply, but when he didn't, Ted said, "That's OK. We'll manage."

Cliff's laughter was whipped from his lips by the brisk, dust-laden wind. "We'll manage!" he sneered. "Can't even harness the mules without help but, 'we'll manage!' That's a big joke."

It seemed as though Mr. Denholm had not even heard his son. His face was gray with concern and his great, rough hands were trembling. He looked out toward the horizon and seemed to be studying the clouds of dust, stirring restlessly over dry fields. Slowly he turned back to the boys. "Better start harrowing the west 40," he said. "I was over there yesterday. It's beginning to blow pretty bad."

Cliff nodded.

"And be careful of those mules," he continued. "They're tricky to harness."

"You don't have to worry about *me*," Cliff snapped. "I know what I'm doin'."

The boys crossed the farmyard together.

"What good does it do to harrow a field this time of year?" Ted wanted to know. "Dad won't be planting for a month or more." The instant he put the question to his stepbrother he realized he had made a mistake.

At the barn door Cliff faced him. "You don't know much, do you?" He shook his head as though it was difficult to believe anyone could be as stupid as Ted. "Harrowing turns the soil over and helps keep it from blowing," he explained. "And it breaks up the clods so the rain can soak in—if we ever get any."

Ted's cheeks flamed. "I'm glad I asked."

The other boy went over to the pegs where the harness was hanging. Ted hesitated, watching him uneasily. "What do you want me to do?"

"You?" Cliff's voice was honed sharp with disgust. "You can watch me or you can start to harness Old Blue. If you should get started, I'll come and help you when I'm through with my team."

Ted winced. He had never worked Old Blue, but he knew the ill-tempered mule by reputation. Like Dad Denholm said, if Old Blue hadn't been able to do the work of three ordinary animals, Dad would have shipped him off to the glue factory long ago.

If a guy wasn't careful, Old Blue would step on his foot or clamp those huge teeth on a hand or shoulder when he was trying to get the harness on the mule. Ever since they moved to the farm, Ted had been afraid of the cantankerous mule, and Cliff knew it.

"Yeah," he taunted, "if you want to do something, you can work on Old Blue."

Just thinking about getting the harness and going into that stall made Ted sweat. But he had to do it. If he didn't, Cliff would never let him hear the last of it.

Grimly he approached the big mule. "Easy, Boy," he said, his voice trembling. "Easy now."

Cliff saw what he was about to do and tried to stop him.

"You'd better leave Old Blue to me. Harnessing that mule is a man's job."

"I know," Ted said quietly. "That's why I'm going to do it." He laid a hand on the mule's back and spoke to him once more, the way he had heard Dad Denholm speak when he was getting ready to harness the mule.

Ted felt the skin under his hand twitch and for a pained instant, he knew something was about to happen. His lips parted but no sound came. The mule knew Ted was inexperienced and sensed that he was afraid as well. Shifting his weight suddenly, the heavy animal leaned toward Ted, trapping him against the stall planking.

"Blue!" he choked, pounding on the mule's back with his fists. "B—" The word caught in his throat, choked off, as the breath was squeezed from his lungs. His head reeled and he felt his knees go weak.

Cliff saw what was happening and sprang to help him. "Blue!" he shouted. He snatched up a small board and hit the mule on the rump. "Blue! Blue! Get over there!"

Ted could scarcely hear him. Cliff's voice sounded faint and far away, as if he were calling through a long tunnel. Ted didn't know how long the mule held him trapped or how Cliff managed to get the animal to shift his weight. But finally Old Blue straightened and Ted fell to his knees.

Cliff grabbed Ted and dragged him back out of the stall. "Are you all right?" Ted heard a familiar voice say from a distance. "Ted, are you all right?"

At first he couldn't speak. A sharp, penetrating pain jabbed his lungs and spread through his body.

"Are you all right?" Cliff repeated.

"I—I—" Finally Ted was able to make a sound.

Cliff managed to get him over to a small pile of hay in the barn and lay him down. For several minutes, Ted fought to breathe while the other boy hovered over him. At last Ted was able to stand again. "Man!" he exclaimed, "I don't want anything like that to happen again."

"Neither do I," Cliff said. "I really didn't mean for you to harness that stupid mule! I—I was just kiddin'." He felt Ted's chest, tenderly. "Are you sure you don't have any broken ribs or anything?"

"I—I think I'm all right," Ted said.

"You'd better sit down again." All the meanness was gone, and for the first time Ted saw genuine concern in the other boy. "Man, that was close!"

Ted wanted to tell Cliff that he was all right and was ready to help him harness the mules and get to work, but his knees were shaky and he was trembling so much he sagged to the hay once more.

"Just stay here while I harness Old Blue," Cliff told him, setting to work cautiously. The mule knew Cliff was the master of the situation. Old Blue stood calmly while he was harnessed, acting so quiet and dependable no one would have believed he was capable of causing trouble.

"I'd better use Old Blue and Jennie Girl myself," Cliff said. "They're a little harder to handle than the other team." Before untying the mules, he left them and went back to where Ted was sitting. "Feel like working now?"

He nodded.

"Good." He acted as though he was about to go to work himself, but he had more to say. "You aren't goin' to tell the old man about this, are you?"

Ted shook his head. "Nope. It's between you and me. I'm not saying anything unless I'm asked, point blank, and have to tell or lie."

After a moment or two of silence, Cliff said, "Know something? You can be an all right guy when you want to."

As they worked that afternoon, Ted pondered Cliff's remark. Did Cliff actually mean what he said, or was he just trying to get Ted to do something for him.

Magicians 7 Compete

SPRING THAT YEAR was hot and dry and windy. The temperature climbed into the upper 90s with maddening regularity the first week in April. Dry dirt drifted into long, sprawling ridges at the fencerows. In some places the cattle could step right over the barbed wire that was supposed to contain them. When they got out, they roamed in all directions, desperate to find green grass.

Clouds drifted across the sky as usual, it seemed to Ted. But nothing came of them. Lightning would flash briefly and they'd hear a roll of distant thunder. Occasionally, a spattering of rain would fall—just enough to dimple the hard dirt driveway.

One night they had half an inch of rain. It came down leisurely, so it all soaked into the thirsty ground. But it wasn't nearly enough to help the crops. Still, it brought a smile to Dad Denholm's eyes.

"Maybe our drought is over," he announced at the supper table. And the next morning, during devotions, they had a time of praise and thankfulness.

Gradually, Ted was learning how to harness the mules alone, hitch them to an implement, and drive them with a minimum of trouble. He also learned to plow a straight furrow. And he learned to scan the western skies for a sign of rain that seldom came.

They were so busy on the farm now that Ted's box of magic lay unopened in his chest. He didn't think of it until Cliff tried to talk him into letting him borrow some of his tricks for the all-school chautauqua in late May.

"Sorry," Ted told him, "but I promised not to show my tricks to anybody or let anybody use them."

"But it's different when it's another magician," Cliff said.

Ted drew a long breath. The tricks were his and as far as he was concerned it didn't make any difference whether it was ethical to loan them to another magician or not. He wasn't going to let anyone use them —especially Cliff.

"You're just jealous because I'm goin' to be in the program and you're not," Cliff said.

"You can think anything you want to, but I don't allow *anybody* to use my tricks," Ted said.

"Especially me—" Cliff said. "Is that it?"

Ted shrugged. "If you want to believe that, nothing I can do will change your mind."

The other boy glared at him, his dark eyes, snapping. "OK!" he blurted. "I'll order a couple of tricks from the catalog I just got." He started out of the room but paused at the door long enough to speak over his shoulder. "I thought maybe you wanted to get along with me, but I can see now that it doesn't make any difference to you."

Ted thought about calling him back and showing him a couple of small tricks he could use if he wanted to. He was sure Uncle Carl wouldn't care. Like Cliff said, the code of ethics was different for other magicians. Besides, he had promised to do everything he could to get along with Cliff. But, why should he try anymore? The only time Cliff was nice to him was when he wanted something, like not telling his dad about the mule-harnessing incident.

* * *

In mid-April, Mrs. Harrison sent a note to Ted. She started by saying that she was having a surprise birthday party for Bart. She planned to invite the entire class, but she had another reason for writing personally to Ted. "Bart and Loren and Dave talked so much about the magic tricks you did for the Rangers," she wrote, "that I'd like to have you give a little program at his party. I don't know of anything Bart would enjoy more."

Ted got out several of his best tricks and practiced until he was able to do them smoothly. Although his sleight-of-hand tricks had lain in the trunk for months, by the day of the party, he was as sharp as he had ever been.

The entire class was invited, including the teacher. Everyone, except a girl who had measles and Cliff, showed up. Cliff met Ted and his friends in the hall at school that afternoon and informed them he wouldn't be there.

"You Rangers didn't want *me* to play basketball with you," he said, bitterly. "You won't want me at the birthday party."

Ted thought Cliff might have heard he was giving the program and stayed home for that reason, but later he decided that wasn't it. Everybody at the house was genuinely surprised when Ted came out and started entertaining them. Miss Winslow, particularly. She sought him out after the party, when he was packing up to go home.

"I didn't know you did magic," she said. "That was a delightful program."

He thanked her, self-consciously.

"Where did you get such tricks and learn to do them so well?"

He told her about Uncle Carl.

"I think that's wonderful," she said. "Would you like to try out for the all-school chautauqua this year, Ted?"

He frowned as he put away the last trick and stood. "I hadn't thought much about it."

"I'm one of the sponsors, Ted," she continued, "and we'll be having tryouts in a week."

"Cliff Denholm does magic too," he reminded her. He knew they wouldn't have two sleight-of-hand acts on the same program.

"I know," she answered, "but I think you'd have a good chance of making it." She acted as if she were about to go further in what she said, but she didn't. She smiled warmly. "You'll try out, won't you?"

At first Ted was uncertain. He'd like to. He knew

he was good and he enjoyed having people clap for him. But if he did make the program, it would only cause a big hassle with his stepbrother. And if he didn't, Cliff would torment him for the rest of his life. Still, the more he thought about it, the more certain he was that he would be chosen to perform.

He had seen Cliff's tricks and they were all right, but they weren't anything exceptional. In fact, most of Cliff's tricks were the kind a beginner did, the kind that could be bought in almost any city.

When Ted got home from school after the party, he called Anne aside and told her what had happened.

When he paused, she said, "Well, what are you going to do?"

"That's what I'm asking you," Ted replied. "What do you think I should do?"

"If you try out, Cliff won't have a chance," Anne said loyally. "You'll beat him."

"Then you think I should?"

"That's something you'll have to decide for yourself."

He stared at a crack in the wall for a long time. Finally he said, "I just might try. If you think I could win."

"You will," she assured him. "And, to tell you the truth, it sounds to me as though Miss Winslow has already made up her mind."

"Of course she's not the only one," Ted said.

"No, but she's on the committee," Anne reminded him.

He went up to his room and began to practice. Now

that he had decided to try out for the chautauqua, he wanted to be as good as possible.

He said nothing to anyone else about his plans, but someone must have talked. Word soon reached Cliff that he was going to have competition for the all-school event. In a night or two he cornered Ted in the barn where they were milking.

"I hear you're trying out against me." Hostility twisted Cliff's broad face.

"Miss Winslow asked me to," Ted replied truthfully, "and I've been thinking some about it."

"I've had it sewed up for the last two years," Cliff boasted. "I hope you know that."

Ted nodded.

"There's no use making such a big deal of it," his stepbrother persisted. "You know how good I am. If you try out, you'll just make a fool of yourself, little brother."

Ted grinned. "I'll take my chances."

"I can tell you right now that I'll beat you," Cliff said.

"That doesn't make any difference. I'm going to give it a try, anyway," Ted said.

"OK," Cliff blustered. "If that's the way you want it, OK!"

At the tryouts the next day, Ted was quietly confident in spite of the fact that his stepbrother did better than he ever had before, according to the judges. When it came time for his own turn, he went to the platform calmly. He began his act with a card trick his uncle Carl had taught him. Then he showed the committee three or four of his best routines and ended with the magical steel rings.

"I'd like to have someone come up and examine them to make sure there's no trickery involved," he began, holding a ring loosely in each hand. "How about you, young man?"

The others snickered as he pointed to the principal, Mr. Anderson. Mr. Anderson came to the platform and pronounced the rings solid. Ted took them and snapped two of them together and did the same with the third and fourth.

All the while he kept talking to his audience, reminding them that a man of the principal's character and integrity had said that the rings were solid. Before he had finished, it was apparent, even to Cliff, that Ted had won.

"I could have beaten you," his stepbrother complained bitterly as they left the building to walk home, "if I'd had somebody give *me* a lot of professional tricks."

Ted faced him and said, "I thought you did OK."

Cliff turned away.

At the supper table that night, both boys were unusually quiet. Anne finally spoke up. "Well," she demanded, "who won?"

Ted pretended not to know what she was talking about.

"Who's going to be in the chautauqua?"

Crimson surged up Cliff's neck. He glared at Anne a moment, then looked down at his plate.

"You'll have the honor of seeing the one and only

Theodore Wills, the world's greatest magician!" Ted said to Anne. Triumph gleamed in his eyes as he watched Cliff.

For a brief instant, silence gripped the family. Then Ted pushed back from the table. "Well, I'd better get upstairs and practice. I've got to polish my act."

"It wasn't fair!" he heard Cliff protest defensively as Ted headed for the stairs. "Ted has all those professional tricks and even had someone teach him how to use them. I had to pick up mine on my own. There was nothing fair about it!"

Getting 8 Even

TED GOT OUT two or three of his tricks and began to go over them carefully, step by step. But he didn't feel much like practicing, at least not right then. In his mind he went over the tryouts of the afternoon, enjoying each moment. For once he had beaten Cliff Denholm and everyone in town would know it. He sat down and leaned back in the chair.

Only the look Dad Denholm gave him as he left the table disturbed the warm, comfortable feeling he'd had since winning a place in the chautauqua. His stepfather hadn't been upset by the fact he had won, Ted was sure. Perhaps he wasn't concerned at all, but the boy thought he saw disapproval in the older man's eyes.

Maybe Dad Denholm didn't like what I said at the table. And maybe I shouldn't have bragged, Ted realized. *I guess it wasn't very Christlike, knifing Cliff that way. But that guy deserved it. After all, he rips into me every chance he gets. He'd have said a lot more, if he had won.*

Ted knew he should apologize to Cliff, but that wouldn't be easy. And Cliff probably wouldn't accept an apology, anyway. He'd never met anyone in his life who could be so disagreeable.

Usually the boys walked to school with Anne and Anita, but the following morning, Cliff hurried through his share of the chores and left the house a full 10 minutes ahead of the others.

"What's the matter with him?" Anne asked, wrinkling her nose. "Doesn't he want to go to school with us?"

Anita's small fingers tightened on her lunch bucket and hurt showed in her eyes. "I think he's mad at Ted," she said. "Cliff was really counting on being in the chautauqua again."

"He had as much chance of making it as I did," Ted told her, suddenly defensive. "If he'd been better than me, he'd have gotten it."

"I know," she replied, "but—"

The tone of her voice bothered him. "But *what?*" he asked.

She shrugged, "Oh, nothing," she said.

"It's not my fault I was chosen in his place," Ted said. "I just entered after the teacher invited me to. The judges picked me."

"I know it isn't your fault, Ted." Anita's eyes were big and luminous. "Just forget it. OK?"

For some reason they walked slower than usual that morning and got to school only moments before the last bell. Ted was sorry about that. He wanted to have time to see Bart and the other Rangers and let them know he was going to be in the chautauqua. But he had to hurry to his homeroom and just made it to his seat as the last bell rang. Miss Winslow frowned in disapproval.

It was not until noon that he was able to see the other boys. As soon as the bell rang, he hurried and caught up with Bart and Loren as they were going out the door.

"Hey!" he called to them. "Wait up!"

They went outside as though they hadn't heard him.

"Hey," he sang out again. "Wait a minute! I've got something to tell you!"

They stopped on the walk and waited, their faces like stone. "Did you have something you wanted to say?" Bart asked him, his young voice cold and unfriendly.

"Yeah, I wanted to tell you that I'm going to—" His voice trailed off as he read the hostility in his friends' faces.

"We couldn't care less what you do or don't do," Bart said.

"And that's the truth!" Loren broke in.

Ted stared from one to the other in bewilderment. "What gives?" he asked. "What'd I do?"

"If you don't know," Loren said, icily. "I'm not goin' to tell you!"

"Come on." Bart touched his companion on the arm. "We haven't got all day!"

Ted took half a step after them, then stopped. It didn't make sense. Bart and Loren were his very best friends. The three of them, with Dave Chandler, had founded the Rangers. They'd played basketball and football and baseball together and were in the same Sunday School class and Boy Scout troup. Like Mrs. Harrison said, if she could find Ted or Loren, she knew Bart had to be somewhere close.

They hadn't even argued and fought like other guys their age did sometimes. At least not very often. They might squabble a little once in a while, but they had never been mad at each other, until now. What was going on?

Ted remained on the sidewalk outside the school building until Bart and Loren turned the corner. Then he trudged back inside to get his lunch box. He found a place on the steps apart from everyone else and got out a sandwich, but he didn't feel like eating. He was still sitting there, his sandwich in his hand, when Cliff came over. "I suppose you've been braggin' to everybody in school about how you beat me out of the chautauqua," he growled.

Ted looked up. "Who cares about that stupid program?" he blurted.

"I thought you did," Cliff said. "You were sure blowin' about it at the house last night."

"Go on," Ted said, miserably. "Just leave me alone."

Cliff straightened, a crooked grin tugging at the corners of his mouth. "I can leave you alone," he said. "You bet I can!" He sauntered away without looking back.

Ted took a couple of bites of the sandwich, but there was no use trying to eat any more. He wasn't hungry. Hurriedly, he put the rest back in his lunch box and went into the school.

He set his lunch box on the floor beneath the hook where his jacket hung. Then he walked the halls, trying to find Bart and Loren. He didn't care whether they wanted to talk to him or not. He had to speak to them and find out what was wrong.

If his friends were in the building, they had to be hiding. He couldn't find them anywhere. Finally, he stationed himself just inside the homeroom door so he could catch them as they came in. Moments before the last bell rang, they pushed angrily past him.

"Bart," he said, grasping his arm, "Bart, I've got to talk to you!"

His friend jerked away. "Keep your hands off me!"

Ted was sick inside as the other boys hurried to their seats. He made his way past the girl with the pigtails who sat behind him and went to his desk. No use trying to talk to those two now. For some reason they had decided to have nothing to do with him. He'd have to find Dave and see what he said about it.

Only it was no easier getting to him than the others. He searched the building as soon as school was out, but he could not track Dave down. By the time he started home, Anne, Anita, and Cliff had already left and he had to walk alone.

When he finally reached home, he was bawled out for being late. But he was so troubled about his friends that the lecture didn't bother him.

The next morning he was at his desk before class when Bart walked up.

"Hi!" Ted exclaimed, his face brightening.

"I've got this for you." Bart laid a folded piece of paper on Ted's desk. "It's from the Rangers."

Bart was so cold and unfriendly, Ted went numb. He unfolded the paper with trembling fingers and read: AT A SPECIAL MEETING OF THE RANGERS LAST NIGHT, YOU, TED WILLS, WERE REMOVED AS PRESIDENT AND VOTED OUT OF THE CLUB.

Signed: Bart Harrison

Loren Derksen

Dave Chandler

Ted's knees almost buckled and he felt sick. They were kicking him out of the club he had thought up. But why?

He read the note again. There had to be some mistake. He hadn't done anything to the other club members. Why would he? They were his friends—his best friends.

If they'd only talk to him, he could find out what he was supposed to have done and get the mess straightened out, but they didn't give him a chance to tell them anything.

Well, if that was the way they wanted to be, let them have their dumb old club. He didn't want to be president, anyway. And they could find someone else to take his place on their basketball team next winter —if they had one.

Let them get Cliff. They had all wanted him last winter. Now they could have him, and they'd soon find out how much trouble he'd cause.

Still, he felt as if he didn't have a friend in the

entire school. The rest of the day was like a bad dream. He had trouble writing a paragraph in English and flunked an unexpected arithmetic test. He should have gotten good grades on both papers. But his mind wouldn't function properly. For that day, at least, he simply didn't care.

At home after supper, he was so quiet that Anne asked curiously, "Don't you feel all right?"

"Sure, I feel OK," Ted answered.

"Then what is it?" she prodded.

He shook his head. "Nothing you can do anything about."

She came over and sat across from him, leaning forward earnestly and lowering her voice. "Would it help to talk about it?"

He shook his head. "Not to *you!*"

He spoke so sharply she took offense. "Well, pardon me for intruding! I just wanted to help! You look like a sick fish!"

She flounced out of the room and he sat, staring at the floor. He had only told her the truth, he reasoned. There was nothing she could do. And the worst of it was, there was nothing he could do either. Bart and Loren and Dave wouldn't listen to him. They wouldn't give him a chance to defend himself.

When he reached school the next day, he was greeted with the news that the Rangers were going to meet him off the school grounds and fight with him. Sid Crawford, who was now a new member of the club, relayed the information. "Bart said he didn't want to talk to you about it himself because he and

Loren and Dave aren't speaking to you."

"But why?" Ted asked. "I haven't done anything to them."

"That's not the way I heard it," Sid said.

Ted hesitated. "I'm not going to fight with them," he said. "They're my best friends."

Sid's eyes narrowed. "Should I tell them you don't want to fight—that you're scared of 'em?"

"I'm not scared," he protested. "I just don't want to fight."

The other boy snorted. "You sound scared to me."

Ted drew in a deep breath. He didn't want to fight the Rangers, but he couldn't have everyone in the school building thinking he was afraid. "OK," he said hoarsely. "You tell them I'll meet them anywhere they say."

That was what Sid had been waiting for. "In the alley behind Schroeder's Bakery. OK?"

He nodded. "Good enough." He was glad they hadn't picked a place where Grandma Mason might see him. If she got wind of his fighting, he would be in a worse mess than he was already.

Ted didn't know how it would be, fighting three guys. He supposed he would have to tangle with Bart first. He was the biggest. Dave was next, so he'd probably be second. And then Loren, if it lasted that long.

Word of the coming fight spread throughout the school. By noon it seemed that everyone knew about it. It turned out that even the teachers had heard the news. Right after lunch all four boys were called to Mr. Anderson's office.

"Now, what's this talk about a fight?" the principal asked.

No one said anything.

"Ted," the principal said sternly, when nobody else spoke, "What's this all about?"

"I don't know," he answered. "Bart gave me a note yesterday morning telling me I was kicked out of the Rangers—that's our club—but I don't know why. Now they've challenged me to fight them, and I still don't know why."

"That's a lie!" Loren blurted.

"Just a minute," Mr. Anderson said, firmly. "Let Ted finish. You'll get your turn later."

"There isn't anything more to tell, except that Sid Crawford came and said the guys wanted to fight me in the alley behind the bakery tonight after school."

"All three of them?" Mr. Anderson asked.

"I guess so," Ted said.

The principal turned to the Rangers. "There's not going to be any fight," he announced, "and especially not three of you against Ted."

"But you ought to hear what he said about us," Bart broke in.

"What did he say?" Mr. Anderson questioned.

"He's been saying we cheated on our tests and were stealing stuff from the grocery store."

Mr. Anderson frowned. "Is that right, Loren?"

Loren nodded.

"And how about you, Dave? Is that true?"

"That's what Ted's been telling people, but we don't cheat or steal."

The principal glanced at his watch. "I've got a class to teach now, so I can't spend any more time on this, but I'll be talking with you boys again in the morning."

"In the hall outside the principal's office, Ted turned to his companions. "I didn't say anything like that about you," he said firmly.

They stared angrily at him.

"But I didn't!" Ted protested.

"Don't lie to us," Bart said. "We know better."

"Yeah," Dave agreed.

"But I wouldn't do that!" Ted protested. "You're my best friends."

"You sure haven't shown it lately!" Bart exclaimed. "You've been bragging and blasting about being president of the Rangers and how that gave you the right to do anything you wanted."

"And you tried your best to get the trophy we won playing basketball so you could keep it for yourself," Dave added.

"And since you've been doing magic, you've been so stuck on yourself you've been acting like you hardly know us," Loren put in.

"I—I—" Ted stammered.

"And now you've been putting us down by telling lies about us and we're not standing for it!" Bart said.

"That's right!" Loren exclaimed. "Old Anderson saved you from getting beat up tonight, but we'll get you! We'll get even if it takes months!"

When 9 Friends Become Enemies

TED WAS THANKFUL he wouldn't have to fight with his friends, but in a way he was more concerned now than he had been before the meeting in the principal's office. Mr. Anderson had an ominous gleam in his eyes when he said he would see them the next morning. Ted was sure the principal hadn't believed him.

When Ted left the building that afternoon, still carrying a chunk of ice in the pit of his stomach, he was glad Cliff had either gone on ahead or was lingering behind. Only Anita and Anne were there to walk home with him. At least he wouldn't have to put up with his stepbrother's taunts for a while.

Ted hadn't planned on saying anything to either of the girls about the proposed fight or the meeting in Mr. Anderson's office. He was hoping they hadn't heard anything about it, so they wouldn't take the story home. But like all the other kids in school, they knew everything. As soon as he joined them for the walk home, they wanted to know what had happened.

He was surprised to find that Anne was so upset, she was wheezing badly.

"I was so worried when I heard that all three of them wanted to fight you, Ted," Anne said, shuddering. "I could hardly study all day just thinking about it."

"I prayed and prayed for you," Anita broke in.

"Well," he said, blushing self-consciously, "there wasn't any fight and there's not going to be any."

Anita's smile was quick. "God answers prayer."

At first he hadn't wanted to talk about it, but now that he had started, he continued, concern edging his voice. "I don't think it's over yet. I'm afraid Mr. Anderson didn't believe me when I told him I hadn't lied about the other Rangers."

"He *has* to believe you!" Anita exclaimed loyally. "You were telling the truth."

"I know I was telling the truth," he said, wishing she was right. But he knew that sometimes people believed a lie instead of the truth. Like right now. Bart and Loren and Dave refused to believe him. They had already decided that he had lied about them and they wouldn't even let him tell them differently.

"Mr. Anderson said he would see us tomorrow," he concluded. "I don't know what's going to happen, but I know it's not going to be good."

"Anne and I will be praying for you," Anita assured him.

Ted expected Cliff to tease him about what had happened at school that day. Strangely, Cliff said little while they were milking, except to ask sarcastically what Ted had to give Mr. Anderson to get him to call off the fight.

"What do you mean?" Ted asked, testily.

"Well," Cliff said, grinning. "Let's put it this way. Old Anderson sure got you off the hook when he said there wasn't going to be any fight. Those guys would have clobbered you!"

Ted went back to his milking without saying anything more. He was thankful he was doing something that allowed him to keep his back to his stepbrother. Perhaps that would help keep Cliff's mouth closed.

That night Ted spent a long time praying about what had happened. He asked God to help him as he faced Mr. Anderson again the next day and prayed that the Rangers would understand that he was telling the truth. He almost wished he were guilty. Then he could confess and ask them to forgive him. At least that way the matter would be over and done with.

The following morning at 10 o'clock, Mr. Anderson sent for Ted. Bart, who was two seats ahead of him, looked back and snickered. Cliff was grinning widely.

Ted was the only one called in. That meant the principal had decided he was guilty. A chill danced nervously down his spine.

Mr. Anderson was standing with his back to the door when Ted entered his small, simply furnished office. He turned slowly, his long face serious. "Ted," he began, "would you like to tell me what happened?"

The boy's voice was shaking so much he had difficulty getting out the words. "I've already told you everything I know. I didn't say anything about the guys. If I was going to talk about anyone, it sure wouldn't be my friends."

The principal sat down across from him, tapping the desk with his pencil. "I'm going to give you one last opportunity to tell me the truth."

Ted took a deep breath. "I don't know what more I can say," he replied, finally. "I've told you everything I know. And, even if you don't believe me, I've told you the truth."

"Ted, I've gone into this matter with the other three, individually," Mr. Anderson went on. "They all tell substantially the same story. I would like to believe you. You've been a good student and haven't caused us any trouble, until now. But I have the word of three who say you are not telling the truth."

Ted remained silent.

"I have decided that as punishment you will not be permitted to take part in the chautauqua," Mr. Anderson said.

Ted nodded miserably. Not that it made any difference one way or the other about the program. The worst thing was having the Rangers turn against him and kick him out. He hadn't done anything against them, yet they had turned on him. They would never be his friends again.

"There's one more thing I must warn you about before you go back to class. If anything like this happens again, you will be suspended. We cannot tolerate a student lying."

He winced at the principal's statement and wondered if he would ever be believed again.

For a week or so now, Cliff had avoided going home with Ted and the girls, but on that particular afternoon he joined them. In fact he had been out in front waiting for them when they left the building.

The afternoon sun had a dull, reddish cast as it hung above the trees on the western horizon. Below it faint gray clouds stretched across the sky. The air was still, so the parched leaves of the cottonwoods and Chinese elms scarcely stirred as the kids hurried along the wide street. Ted struck out with a strong stride, hoping Cliff would fall behind and leave him alone, but that was not to happen. He had scarcely reached the street before his stepbrother was beside him.

"Things are really workin' out great," Cliff said, expansively. "Aren't they?"

Ted's lips tightened at the scorn in the other boy's voice. "What do you mean?"

"Well, Anderson stopped the fight so you didn't get all messed up, for one thing. I wouldn't have wanted to see that. It would have been terrible to have you come home with a black eye and a crooked nose. 'Nita and Anne might even have cried when they saw you."

"Leave me alone, will you?" Ted muttered.

"Don't be so upset. I'm just naming the things you've got to be thankful for—like not gettin' suspended for the lies you told about your precious Rangers."

Ted glanced quickly at him, suddenly suspicious. "How do you know so much?"

They cut diagonally across an intersection and

made their way west a block to the road that led them to the Denholm farm.

"I just know," Cliff said, impishly. "Like I know you're not goin' to be in the chautauqua the way you thought you'd be."

Neither of the boys was aware that the girls were close enough to hear what they were saying until Anita broke in. "Cliff!" she exclaimed. "Please don't be like that."

Jerking around, Cliff faced her. "Whose *sister* are you, anyway?" he demanded.

"I just don't like to hear you making fun of Ted all the time," she said.

His laughter was coarse. "I'm not making fun of him. I just wanted to tell him that we're keepin' the magic act in the family. They came and asked *me* to do it, now that Mr. Anderson has decided that Ted would be a disgrace to the school if he got up and showed off his uncle's tricks."

Ted wished Anita would keep quiet, but she was determined to let her brother know he was wrong.

"I don't believe it," she told him. "I know Ted. He wouldn't do what they say he did."

"That's the way you are! Sticking up for a guy who lied about his best friends and got in trouble for it," Cliff persisted. "Go ahead, 'Nita. Ask him. If he tells you the truth, he'll admit he got the boot from Old Anderson this morning."

"I don't care about that," she countered. "I still don't believe he did it. Telling things about his friends that weren't true, I mean."

Ted appreciated her loyalty, but he realized it wouldn't do any good. Anne and Anita were probably the only kids in the school who didn't believe the stories about him.

He glanced up at the sky. A shimmering curtain seemed to have dimmed the sun. And a breathless hush had settled over the countryside, like the stillness before a storm.

"We'd better hurry," Ted said aloud. "It looks like it's going to rain."

"Sure!" Cliff laughed contemptuously. "Change the subject so you don't have to tell them *I'm* takin' over." He directed his attention to Anne. "Miss Winslow came and asked *me* to be in the chautauqua with my magic act. She said she had to have my answer right away because they're having a big supper meeting over at the Bergman place across the fields from us tonight to make the final arrangements."

The girls eyed him, but said nothing.

"I felt like tellin' her they could go jump, but I finally took pity on them," Cliff went on, "seeing as how it was my very own stepbrother who let them down."

Anne's cheeks reddened and her eyes were hard as steel. Her wheezing was growing worse. Watching her, Ted felt a twinge of concern. It was things like this, almost as much as a cold or the weather, that threw her into a severe asthma attack.

"It's OK, Anne," he said quickly. "Don't let it get to you. We can't do anything about it."

She was so disturbed, she scarcely listened. "You've never thought about anyone else but yourself in your whole life, Cliff," she said. "Don't try to tell us you felt sorry for *anybody*."

Cliff winced, and for an instant Ted thought he saw hurt in the other boy's eyes. But when his stepbrother spoke, there was no trace of anything other than contempt in his voice.

"I just *love* Little Brother," Cliff said. "Besides, I have too much of the old school spirit to leave the chautauqua in a hole. Do you know what people said after last year's program? They told me it would have been a frost—a complete wipeout—if it hadn't been for my act. I saved the show."

"I'll bet!" Anne replied, angrily.

Ted turned away, clenching his fists. They walked on for a short distance before Cliff sidled closer to him. "There's something I've been wanting to ask you," he said, the sting gone from his voice.

Ted waited, warily, for him to continue.

"How about lettin' me borrow a couple of your uncle's tricks?"

Ted looked at him in unbelief. "You think I'd give you any of my tricks after all you've said?"

"I won't hurt 'em," Cliff said.

"You're crazy!" Ted replied. "I already told you nobody uses my magic stuff, so forget it!"

Cliff glared at him. "If I were you," he warned, "I'd think a couple of times before turning a guy like me down."

They had stopped walking and stood, toe to toe, staring each other down. "Maybe you'd better tell me just what you mean by that!" Ted demanded.

"You know!" Cliff said.

"Spell it out," Ted insisted.

"I warned you about beatin' me out of the chautauqua," he blurted, "but you wouldn't listen!"

Ted caught his breath sharply. Suddenly the pieces fell into place. "So you're the one who told Bart and the guys all those lies!"

"Maybe I did," Cliff replied.

"I'm going right back and talk to them." Ted glanced toward town.

"Go ahead," Cliff blustered. "But I can tell you one thing right now. You'd better be home to help me with the chores tonight or the old man'll clean your plow!"

Ted hesitated. Dad Denholm and his mom had said something about going into town that afternoon to see Grandma Mason and that they might stay for supper. If he walked back to Elmville now, he would be leaving all the chores for Cliff. His stepfather would be upset about that. He didn't like having either of the boys shirk their responsibilities at home.

"I'll talk to the Rangers tomorrow," he said.

The bigger boy cocked his fist and took half a step toward Ted. "You won't talk to nobody!" he snarled.

Anita must have seen his threatening manner. "Cliff!" she cried. "Don't you dare fight with Ted."

He grinned and stepped back, lowering his huge hand. "Don't worry, I ain't goin' to hurt Little Brother." His voice dropped to a whisper. "As long as he does what I say."

Before Ted had a chance to reply, Cliff loped off.

When Ted and the girls reached the farm, Cliff

already had the cows in their stalls and was starting to milk. "Figured I'd just as well get going," he said with surprising friendliness when Ted entered the barn. "The weather acts sort of funny and the cows are restless, like they get when a bad storm's on the way."

Ted nodded. The sky was darkening and the dying sun cast a reddish hue across the farmstead. It was far too early for it to be dark, but it looked as if sunset was almost upon them. The sun rested on the tip of what seemed to be a cloud in the west.

Ted picked up a milk stool from the far end of the barn, and the pail Cliff had brought out for him. He took another quick look at the distant horizon and was standing motionless when the other boy called out to him. "You can't milk cows over there."

Ted moved quickly back to his first animal and set to work, taking out his anger and frustration on the even-tempered holstein who munched her cud calmly, waiting for him to finish. He moved to the next cow, milking mechanically from months of practice.

The boys didn't talk to each other as they worked, but when they were almost done, they chanced to be emptying their pails in the 10-gallon milk can at about the same time.

"Ted," Cliff said, defensively. "You've got the wrong idea about me. I didn't tell the Rangers anything about you. I don't know where they got the idea you started stories about them, but I can tell you this much. It didn't come from me."

"Then you won't care if I check it out with them," Ted said.

Cliff Denholm shifted nervously from one foot to the other. "Those guys don't like me," he went on. "They just might say it was me in order to get me in trouble."

"They wouldn't do that." Ted set the pail down and looked out the open door at the sky once more. In the short time they had been in the barn milking, it had grown measurably darker. A hushed, eerie feeling settled over the farmstead.

"Can't you take my word that I didn't tell them anything?" his companion demanded.

The muscles in Ted's shoulders tightened. "Why should I?"

Cliff's temper flared. "OK! Go ahead! Talk to them! See if I care! They won't tell you anything! There's nothing to tell!"

They went back to work and had almost finished milking when the storm burst upon them without warning. It was strange the way the storm had come up. One moment everything was quiet—breathlessly still—like a church on Sunday morning before the people arrive. The next instant, the wind was roaring over the prairies, rattling the barn doors, and shaking the building.

But it was not a rainstorm. Far from it. Dust was everywhere, filtering under the doors and around the windows—dust as fine as flour and as thick as snow in a blizzard. A fit of coughing seized Ted.

"Man!" Cliff exclaimed. "What's happening?"

"A dust storm!" Ted cried. He had read about dust storms in Oklahoma and western Kansas but had never thought they'd have one.

"We'd better finish this milking and get to the house before it gets worse!" Cliff warned.

The boys milked the last three cows, finished feeding the small dairy herd and the mules, and set out for the house. At the barn door, they hesitated briefly. Dust was surging through the air—great, billowing clouds of it. The fine, powdery dirt choked them and set them to coughing. After a moment or two, the storm seemed to ease slightly and they could make out the shape of the farmhouse.

"Let's go!" Ted cried.

Bending low, they dashed for the house. They reached the backyard gate just as the clouds of dust closed in again.

"Hurry!" Panic edged Cliff's voice as he tried to push Ted away so he could loosen the gate latch himself. When it opened, they both crushed through for the final 8 or 10 long, running steps to the kitchen door.

Once inside, Ted leaned against the kitchen table for a minute or more, his chest heaving. Cliff sagged to a chair nearby and for a time they were conscious only of the ache in their lungs and the trembling weakness of their knees.

Gradually Ted became aware of the dust that was seeping into the house. A thin film already covered the kitchen table and the cabinet around the sink. There was dust on the window sills and floor. He reached out mechanically and traced his initials in the dirt that covered the oilcloth on the table. It was then that he saw the note on the cloth almost directly in front of him.

"Here's a letter, Cliff," he said.

"Nobody writes to me," answered Cliff.

"Hey, it's to both of us." Ted picked it up and opened it. "It's from 'Nita and Anne!"

Cliff turned quickly and looked around. "They aren't here, are they?"

"They've gone over to the Bergmans'," Ted continued.

"Bergmans'!" Cliff sounded worried and he brushed a hand across his face, uneasily. "What for?"

"Read it for yourself," Ted said, handing it to Cliff.

He took the note and scanned it, his face turning white. It took him so long, he must have gone over it a couple of times, Ted decided. "What'd you do, Little Brother?" Cliff said finally. "Fill them full of lies about me?"

"I didn't even mention you to them," Ted answered.

Cliff pulled in a deep breath and read the note once again—aloud, this time. "SUPPER IS IN THE ICE BOX. WE SET THE TABLE FOR YOU. WE'VE GONE OVER TO BERGMANS' TO TELL MISS WINSLOW AND MR. ANDERSON THE TRUTH ABOUT WHAT HAPPENED BETWEEN TED AND THE RANGERS. WE BOTH KNOW YOU DIDN'T LIE ABOUT THEM, TED. Signed ANITA AND ANNE."

There was a long silence, then Cliff exploded. "You lied to me! You did so talk to them about me!"

"Anything they got about you they got from you," Ted reminded him, testily.

The other boy leaned forward angrily. "If I find out you're behind this, you'll be sorry!" he grated. "And that's a promise!"

Caught 10 in a Dust Storm

THE HOWLING WIND grew stronger yet, enveloping the house in a monstrous black mantle that shut out the sun and made the building as dark as midnight. Ted knew Cliff was in the kitchen with him, but he couldn't see him.

"Get the light!" Ted cried hoarsely.

Cliff stumbled over a chair, knocking it half across the room as he reached for the switch. He fumbled along the wall for an instant or two before locating it. The 60 watt bulb in the middle of the ceiling labored feebly to chase the darkness away. But the corners were still hidden in the shadows.

"There!" Ted exclaimed, forcing the breath from his lungs. "That's better."

Cliff picked up the chair, frowning as he saw the dust on his hands. For the moment his anger subsided. "I sure hope the folks didn't start home and get caught in this," he murmured.

Suddenly Ted thought of the two girls. "They're not the ones I'm worried about."

Cliff came around to face him. "What do you mean by that?"

"Our sisters might be out there!" Ted exclaimed.

"They should have made it without any trouble," Cliff said. "They had less than a mile to go."

"If they got started right away," Ted added. "And if Anne's asthma didn't flare up in this dust. She was wheezing, even before we got home." He shuddered. "If she got caught out in this storm, she'd have such a bad attack she wouldn't be able to breathe— let alone make it to Bergmans'." He started for the phone. "I'm going to call and see if they got there."

Cliff jumped in front of him, anger and fear in his face. "You aren't worried about your sister," he snapped. "You just want to find out if they made it and told Mr. Anderson and Miss Winslow their lies about me!"

"Listen, I don't care about that!" Desperation gripped Ted. "I've got to find out about Anne! You don't know what those asthma attacks are like! She could die!"

Still Cliff Denholm didn't move. "You're not touchin' that phone!"

Ted's fists tightened until the cords stood out on the backs of his hands. "I've got to!"

"You've got to do nothin'!" He put his hands on the smaller boy's chest and shoved him back a step or two.

Tears filled Ted's eyes. "I don't want to fight you, Cliff!"

"Fight me? Ha! I'd clobber you with one hand!"

Ted moved forward, fists cocked. "Then you're going to have to! I'm using that phone!"

Cliff hesitated uncertainly, then stepped back. "If I lay a hand on you," he said, "the old man'll murder me!"

Ted moved to the phone, rang two shorts and a long and asked Mr. Bergman if Anita and Anne had gotten there. He listened a moment, and his lower jaw went slack as he put the receiver back on the hook.

"Are they there?" Cliff asked, showing concern for the first time.

"The Bergmans haven't seen anything of them!" Ted reported. He crossed to the kitchen window quickly and stared out at the thick, blowing dust. The wind didn't seem quite as strong as it had been a few minutes before. He could make out the heavy wire fence and occasionally the faint outline of the barn. Yet the storm was far from over.

Cliff joined him at the window. "What're we going to do?" he demanded.

"Go out after them! Anne's in bad trouble!" Ted said.

"You don't know that!" Cliff countered.

"But I do!" Ted insisted. "I've seen her asthma attacks. A lot less dust than this would knock her out— especially when she was already wheezing." He pulled in a deep, trembly breath. "We've got to find our sisters!"

There was fear in Cliff's eyes. "We can't do that in a storm like this!"

"We have to!" Ted said, moving toward the door.

"We couldn't make it a hundred yards on foot!" Cliff shouted.

Ted sent up a desperate, silent prayer to God for help. "I've got to try. You can come along if you want to."

"I can't let you go alone," Cliff said, following him. "We'll go out to the barn and bridle Old Blue. We'll have a better chance, riding him."

Ted was about to fling the outside door open when he stopped and turned toward Anne's bedroom.

"Where're you going?" Cliff called.

"For her medicine," Ted said. "She'll need it bad."

He found her medications, stuffed them in his pocket, and followed Cliff out, across the broad yard to the barn.

Cliff quickly bridled Old Blue. "Why don't we take one of the others too?" Ted asked, uneasily. He still didn't trust the bad-tempered mule.

"Old Blue's the only one broke to ride," Cliff said.

Ted looked at the mule doubtfully as Cliff led him out into the storm.

The wind had let up quite a bit by now, but gusts of choking dust still blotted out everything. At times, Ted could make out the trees that lined the lane as well as a short stretch of fence that enclosed the pasture between their farm and the Bergman place.

Cliff led Old Blue along the corral gate and vaulted to his back. The skin on the mule's withers quivered. For an instant, it seemed to Ted that Blue's ears were going back, a sure sign of impending trouble.

"Are you OK?" he asked Cliff.

"I'm as OK as I'll ever be."

"How about Old Blue?" Ted asked.

"You c'n ask him if you want to. If he doesn't like it, he'll let us know soon enough."

"That's what I'm afraid of," Ted said grimly.

Old Blue fiddle-footed impatiently when Ted climbed up on the gate and eased his weight on the mule's back behind Cliff. Momentarily the mule seemed uncertain as to whether or not to lower his head and hunch up to buck. Cliff tightened his grip on the reins and smacked him sharply with a small stick he had picked up for that purpose.

The mule took a half-hearted hop that could have been a prelude to a greater effort to unseat his riders. But he seemed to change his mind as a sharp blast of wind sent the dust swirling around them. For a brief instant they sat motionless, unable to see. Then Cliff clucked again to the mule, switched it once more, and the animal broke into a fast trot.

They made their way across the pasture in a zig-zag path, and the boys peered in every direction for some sign of the girls. The dust storm danced a minuet across the pasture, sending clouds of dirt swirling, stopping, and surging forward again. Cliff and Ted had almost reached the far corner of the pasture when Ted caught a glimpse of Anita and Anne huddled together along the fence.

"There they are!" he shouted.

At first Cliff didn't see them and was about to ride on, but Ted punched him in the back. "No!" he cried. "Over there!"

The dust billowed across the pasture as Cliff whirled Old Blue about, but they were able to get over to the girls. They swung off the mule quickly and Cliff loosed the reins. He only relaxed his grip for an instant, but that was enough for alert Old Blue. With a jerk of his head, the mule reared and whirled, twisting free and dashing back to the barn.

Tears trembled in Anita's soft eyes. "W—we got caught in the storm and—and Anne started coughing so bad she—she couldn't go on. She's hardly been able to breathe!" Anita wiped her eyes with the back of her hand. "And the dust was so thick I couldn't see anything. I was afraid Anne was going to die before we could get help—I prayed so hard that God would send someone—and He did!"

Ted barely heard her. He was scarcely aware of the fact that the mule had escaped. Tenderly, he knelt beside his sister. She was lying so still and white! "Anne," he murmured, "are you all right?"

She opened her eyes and her mouth twitched feebly. She tried to answer him but the effort sent her into a fit of coughing.

Ted glanced over at Cliff. "Can you help me?" he asked. "We've got to move her right away."

"Old Blue bolted for the barn," Cliff announced, as though Ted wasn't aware of it. "But we can carry her. We must be close to the Bergman place."

Ted was going to help him but the bigger boy picked Anne up effortlessly, and started forward, using the fence as a guide. Ted took Anita's hand and they stumbled after. At times the dust was so thick they

couldn't even see each other. At other times the blowing eased enough for them to make out the barn and house they were approaching.

Mr. and Mrs. Bergman and their daughter, Denise, must have been at a window. The exhausted little group barely reached the corral when Mr. Bergman rushed out and took Anne from Cliff's arms.

From that moment on, the capable farm couple took over. Mrs. Bergman turned down the quilts on the spare bed and helped Anne get into it. She gave her some of the medication Ted had brought, then lit the Asthmador powder near her head. Anne's breathing was shallow and labored but Ted thought it had eased a little. She didn't have to fight so desperately for breath.

"D—do you think she'll be all right?" he asked, nervously.

Mrs. Bergman nodded.

"Should we phone the doctor?" he said.

The older woman put an arm on his shoulder. "Why don't we wait a short while and see how she is?" she suggested. "I have a feeling that the medicine you brought will help her."

Mrs. Bergman phoned the Denholm house. When she couldn't get their parents, she called them at Grandma Mason's where they had been trapped by the storm. She told them where the children were and that they would keep them overnight.

Anita shared Denise's room, and Mrs. Bergman made a bed for the boys on the living room floor. Ted was already lying down when Cliff brought up the subject of the school principal and Miss Winslow to Ted. "I thought they were supposed to be here for supper and a big meeting," he said.

"Didn't you hear Mrs. Bergman talking to Mom?" Ted asked. "She said they had been expecting company from town but the storm had kept them home."

Cliff went over and switched off the light. For a moment or two he remained motionless. Then he came over and sat down on the blankets beside Ted. "Listen, Ted," he said. "I want you to know that I don't blame you if you go to see Mr. Anderson about all the trouble I caused you. I deserve it."

Ted rolled onto his back and sat up. "I'm not going to see him," he said quickly.

"But I'm the one who was responsible for this trouble," Cliff confessed. "I guess in the first place, when Dad remarried, I was afraid you'd take my place with him."

"I could never do that, even if I wanted to," Ted exclaimed. "Your dad loves you."

"I began thinking while I was walking along with Anne—about a lot of things," Cliff said. "You see, when you came out to the farm, I got next to Dave Chandler at school. Later I found out that you were the president and that I'd have been on the Rangers' team and all—if it hadn't been for you—"

Ted felt miserable as he thought about Cliff's words. So Dave was the informer! But why? Well, right now Ted had his own guilt problem. "It *was* my fault," he admitted. "I sure haven't been proud of it. I was just stupid."

"Well," Cliff went on, "I got so mad about that and the fact you beat me out of the chautauqua. When I found out the guys were upset with you for throwing your weight around as president of the Rangers, I just took advantage of it."

"What do you mean?" Ted asked.

"I told them you'd been lying about them. I swore I'd heard you say all those things they accused you of. I think they believed me because they were jealous of you."

Ted was silent while the clock chimed midnight. He was tempted to deny that he'd been throwing his weight around, as Cliff had said. But he realized suddenly that it was true. Not only that, he had boasted about his magic tricks and the fact that he'd beaten Cliff. No wonder Dave had turned informer!

"I wouldn't blame you if you went to the guys and Mr. Anderson and told them what I did to you," Cliff repeated. "I deserve it."

Ted ran his hand over his face. "I'm not going to."

"Why not? They'll take you back in the Rangers, and you'll get to be in the chautauqua and everything," Cliff said.

Ted leaned forward. "You helped me find Anne and get her here. I owe you a lot for that."

"It was my fault the girls came here in the first place," Cliff admitted. "While we were out there, I saw how selfish I'd been. I thought maybe God was punishin' me and would let Anne die. I know I haven't acted like I care about her—or you, but I guess I do."

"You've confessed to me," Ted told him, tears running down his cheeks in the dark. "Now, I've got something to say to you. The trouble you and I have had has been as much my fault as yours. Maybe more. I haven't treated you right since we came out here. I thought I was so much better than you and—and I haven't treated you the way a Christian should—or the way I ought to treat—my brother."

Cliff was silent.

"And you were right about my keeping you off the team. The other guys said you were so good they wanted you right away. You were their first choice."

"I was?" Cliff broke in with amazement in his voice. "Dave told me they would have taken me on the team if it hadn't been for you. But I didn't know I was their first choice," Cliff said. "Man, I didn't know that. But why are you telling me all this?"

Ted looked over toward the dark hulk that was Cliff. "I guess it hit me like it hit you while we were out there in that storm. When you were carrying Anne and I was helping Anita, I realized for the first time we are really and truly brothers and sisters. I'm ashamed of the way I've been treating you."

"You really mean that?" Cliff said quietly.

"I'm going to talk to the Rangers. If they'll take me back, I'll try to get you in too. We need you in the club and on the basketball team."

"I can't believe it!" Cliff exclaimed.

At that moment Mr. Bergman called from his bedroom, telling them to go to sleep so they could get up the next morning. Cliff turned toward Ted and whispered. "I'm sorry for the way I've treated you too," he said. "I'm going to Mr. Anderson myself and tell him the truth. You deserve to be in the chautauqua, not me."

"I'll go with you then," Ted said. "When I tell him how it happened—the whole story—maybe he'll understand. And you know, he just might let both of us be in the program. We could do a magic act—together!"

Cliff was silent.

Ted said, "I'll share some of my tricks with you. Uncle Carl won't mind."

They continued to whisper for a few minutes. Then they rolled over and closed their eyes. Ted, however, was unable to go to sleep right away. He prayed, asking God to forgive him for all the trouble his proud, angry spirit had caused. Then he prayed for Cliff. His stepbrother wasn't a Christian now, but Ted was sure it wouldn't be long until Cliff would confess his sins to the Lord too, and receive forgiveness.

Until that happened, Ted would pray regularly for him as he'd promised Anita and Dad Denholm. Tomorrow he had to make things right with the Rangers. From now on, with God's help, he'd treat them as equals—as real friends.

It had been a wonderful day!